Ideals and Moral Lessons

FROM

Actual Occurrences

Compiled as Vol. III

OF THE

BOYS AND GIRLS' FIRESIDE SERIES

By A. L. BYERS

D1218654

PREFACE

The Boys and Girls' Fireside Series is an arrangement, in permanent form, of many excellent and interesting narratives, trips and adventures, little sermons, Bible stories, descriptions of nature, various industries and foreign customs, bits of biography and history, missionary experiences, little poems, etc., that have appeared from time to time in the SHINING LIGHT, a periodical for children. Comparatively few who are now in the transitory period of childhood have ever read them, and it is believed that in this permanent form they will be preserved as a treasure-store of useful reading in which boys and girls will find both pleasure and profit.

CONTENTS

CONTENTS

Prov. 4:23-27

IDEALS AND MORAL LESSONS

THE MAN IN THE BOY

In the acorn is wrapped the forest;
  In the little brook, the sea;
The twig that will sway with the sparrow today
  Is tomorrow's sturdy tree;
There is hope in a mother's joy,
  Like a peach in its blossom furled;
And a noble boy, a gentle boy,
  A manly boy, is king of the world.

The power that will never fail us
  Is the soul of simple truth;
The oak that defies the stormiest skies
  Was upright in its youth;
The beauty no time can destroy
  In the pure young heart is furled;
And a worthy boy, a tender boy,
  A faithful boy is king of the world.

The cub of the royal lion
  Is regal in his play;
The eaglet's pride is as fiery-eyed
  As the old bird's, bald and gray;
The nerve that heroes employ
  In the child's young arm is furled;
And a gallant boy, a truthful boy,
  A brave, pure boy, is king of the world.
                              —Anonymous.

THE MANLY BOY

A MANLY boy is one who shows good, manly qualities. We do not expect him to be as large as a man, as strong as a man, nor as wise as a man; but he will be truthful, honest, and well-behaved. He will never speak of his father as "governor" or the "old man," nor will he speak of his mother as the "old woman." He will not be ashamed to have it known that he loves both his father and his mother;

9

nor will he be afraid of all the ridicule that silly boys may heap upon him because of his love. They may call him a baby, and say what they please about his being led by his mother's "apron-strings"; he does not mind that, for he knows he is right.

He will never engage in low, mean sport. He loves real sport, but will do nothing for fun that he would be afraid to talk about at the table. He does not torment small boys, but is ready to help them when he can. His sisters are not careful to hide their work, their books, or their toys from him, lest he should destroy them; he would never think of that. He is careful not to be greedy at the table or rude in company, but remembers that others have rights as well as he himself.

Does anybody say that this is all very well to talk about but that no one has ever yet seen such boys as are here described? We answer, "There are such boys, and we have seen them." They are as full of fun as others; they equal anybody at the different sports in which boys delight; they swim and skate and play ball and roll hoops and run just like other boys, but their behavior is gentle and kind.

The manly boys when they grow up will be, in the best sense of the word, gentlemen. —*Exchange.*

TRUE BRAVERY

WHEN the time came to award the prize every one listened with breathless interest, for the records of two boys were so close that it was impossible to predict who would win. When the suspense was over, the boy who had hoped to be the winner but had lost by only a few points walked over and congratulated the happy winner, and the crowd cheered. It is hard for grown people to give up gracefully, and for a boy of thirteen to be so brave in public was remarkable, and the grown people were as generous with their applause as they had been when the prize was awarded. It would not be telling the truth to say the loser was not disappointed, for he was; but he had himself so well in hand that neither then nor later did he complain or utter the familiar cry, "It wasn't fair!"

Sometimes boys and girls get the idea that no one is brave unless he saves a life or does some striking deed to benefit others. There are boys and girls who are always looking and longing for a chance to save life or to distinguish themselves by some other brave act, but who are daily and hourly ignoring chances to be truly brave.

One of the bravest acts a girl has ever done was unnoticed except by her teacher, who never mentioned to the girl that she saw it. Amy P—— was invited to go to a nutting party with her school friends, but her mother said she must first prepare her lesson for the next day. Her mother was called away from home, and on account of some accident Amy was unable to find time to work her ten tedious problems. The other girls coaxed her to go, saying they were sure it would be all right with her mother; but Amy was firm. Finally one of the girls who wrote very much as Amy did handed her a sheet on which the problems were neatly worked out, and said, "Here, sign your name, and the teacher will never know the difference." It was a great temptation, for Amy knew she was able to work all the problems, as they were only tedious, not hard; but she bravely put it aside and remained at home. Was not that a brave deed for a girl of twelve?

It does not come to every one to have the chance of winning honors by some striking deed of bravery, but there are opportunities even for boys and girls to prove that they are not cowards. Over and over again we must fight our battles when we are young, to be fit for the harder warfare by and by. A very wicked person or a very worthless one might, in an emergency, save many lives; but none except brave, strong men and women win in the great battles of life by keeping their hearts pure and their hands clean, and this calls for the truest and best courage of all.

A FAILURE THAT LED TO SUCCESS

IT DID seem too bad when she met with that serious accident. It caused a big veto to be written across all her plans for the future. She was only fourteen years old, and had just entered the factory as a worker. One day in an unguarded moment the machinery caught her, and dropped her to the floor a mangled, senseless heap.

Six months later she left the hospital a well girl, but with her right arm missing, for it had been crushed so badly that amputation had been necessary. Now what could she do? No more factory life was possible to her. Everything must be changed.

But everything was not ended. A new life opened up to her. During her illness at the hospital she had been often observed by a charitable woman who frequented that place, and her air of intelligence impressed the woman greatly. Hearing of the girl's misfortune, the woman decided that since the girl's livelihood could no longer depend upon the use of her hand, she should have a chance to develop along other lines. So through this woman's influence the girl was sent to school.

And this was the beginning of her new life. She enjoyed her studies and progressed rapidly. A few years later she graduated from high school and was sent to one of the leading women's colleges of the East. Here, when her course was finished, she stood at the head of her class. And now she holds a responsible position in a large educational institution.

The success of this young lady was built upon the seeming failure at the beginning of her life-work. When she saw her plans overthrown, she did not conclude that her defeat was final, but set about to fit herself for another place. And by steady upward strides she won. One writer has said that "God's goodness manifests itself to us often in the garb of disappointment and denial, and we must wait to see how the closing of one door opens the way into higher joy and larger opportunity. But of one thing we may be sure, no defeat is meant to be final, and every seeming failure may be used to build up a larger, more splendid success."

HONESTY IN A CHILD

IN A country school there was a large class standing to spell. In the lesson there was a very hard word. The teacher put the word to the scholar at the head of the class, and he missed it. The word was passed to the next, and the next, and so on through the whole class, till it came to the last pupil, the smallest of the class, and he spelled it right; at least, the teacher understood it so, and the boy went to the head of the class of eighteen boys and girls.

The teacher then turned around and wrote the word on the blackboard, so that they might all see how it was spelled, and learn it better. But no sooner was the word written upon the board than the little boy at the head of the class cried out, "Oh, I didn't say it so; I said e instead of i," and he went back to the foot of his own accord, quicker than he had gone to the head. Was not he an honest boy? The teacher would always have thought he spelled the word right if he had not told her; but he was too honest to take any credit that did not belong to him.

—Selected.

YOUR NICHE

There's a niche for you in the world, my boy,
 A corner for you to fill,
  And it waits today
  Along life's way
For the boy with a frank "I will."
  So, lad, be true;
  The world wants you
In the corner that you may fill.

There's a niche in the world for you, my girl,
 A corner for you to fill,
  For a girl that is kind,
  With a pure, sweet mind,
A place that it waiting still.
  So, lass, be true;
  The world wants you
In the corner that you may fill.

There's a niche for you both in the world, my dears,
 A corner for you to fill,
  And a work to do
  Which no one but you
In God's great plan can fulfil.
  So, dears, be true;
  The world wants you,
And your place is waiting still.

—Selected.

THE WINSOME GIRL

THE winsome girl has a warm, loving heart. She feels "smiley" inside, and the smiles just shine out. She does not think about herself. She does not stand about moping, waiting to be coaxed into a game. She does not take offense when none was intended. She does not imagine that other girls are slighting her. She does not always want to be first.

The winsome girl does not hang her head and refuse to reply when strangers or older people speak to her, but answers as sweetly

and politely as possible. She may be bashful, and her heart may go thumpety-thump in the presence of strangers, but she is never rude or surly on that account. She is brave enough to do hard things, and talking to strangers is a very hard thing for a naturally bashful girl.

The winsome girl never sulks. She is not the sort that never has opinions, but she does not become angry with those who differ from her. If she can not agree with her companions, she does not try to compel them to agree with her.

The winsome girl is—just winsome, that is all. Keep your eyes open, and you will find her some time. Keep sweet, and other folks may find her when they look at you! And that would be best of all.
—*Selected.*

A LESSON FROM THE DANDELION

ONE bright, beautiful spring morning a lady took a walk in the woods. She sat down to meditate upon the goodness of God in giving such a lovely world to his children. She thought, "How happy we should be in this life while preparing for the life in the world to come!"

The trees had put forth their new leaves and were sheltering happy birds that hopped among the branches and sang praises to their Creator. No king's palace was ever furnished with a more elegant carpet than the soft green grass beneath her feet, dotted here and there with the purple violets and Mayflowers.

Ere long her attention was called to a little well-known plant growing near by. It was the dandelion. There he stood, not with his sunny golden head, but with his head already turned to snowy white. His short life was fast drawing to a close. The soft breeze caught up some of his white locks that were ready to fall and bore them away. A gust of wind carried others away and still others, until at last the dandelion stood quite shorn. His work was done. All that was left would soon molder back to earth and be forgotten.

But what about the little seeds among the white locks that had been carried away by the breeze? Some of them fell not far away; while others sailed and sailed in the air and fell nobody knows where, there to take root and grow into other plants.

"Just so it is with our lives," thought the lady. "Though we shall live here but a brief period of time and may be seen by few people, yet our influence will reach here and there and far away because of our words and deeds, when we have returned to dust and have been forgotten."
—*Belle M. Watson.*

TO A LITTLE MAID

How should little maidens grow
  When they're ten or over?
In the sunshine and the air,
Wholesome, simple, fresh, and fair
As the bonnie daisies blow,
  And the happy clover.

How should little lassies speak
  At this time of living?
As the birds do, and the bees,
Singing through the flowers and trees,
Till each mortal fain would seek
  Joy her lips are giving.

How about her eyes and ears
  At this stage of growing?
Like the clear, unclouded skies,
Not too eager or too wise,
So that all she sees and hears
  May be worth the knowing.

And the little maiden's heart?
  Ah! for that we're praying,
That it strong and pure may grow;
God, who loveth children so,
Keep her from all guile apart,
  Through life's mazes straying!
                    —*The Children's Friend.*

CRUTCHES FOR BY AND BY

"MY YOUNG friend, you are fashioning a crutch for by and by," said a college professor to one of his students, who was forming the bad habit of using dishonest helps in doing his work. "The time will come when you will find you can not walk without it. The result of such methods is to make one incapable, in the end, of doing an honest and thorough piece of work, for himself or any one else."

What the professor said was true and just. Every bad habit we form is a crutch for the future. It enfeebles us by depriving us of the power to do right. The dishonest job is a crutch—a poor makeshift for right and fair dealing with others. As the habit of dishonest work grows upon us we lose the power to walk with vigorous uprightness in the pathway of human service.

So it is with every bad habit: it takes away our capability for living rightly. The evil personal habit in time makes us incapable of living normally. With what a wretched crutch the drunkard, for example, has to hobble through life! How he literally chains himself to it! and what a pitiful spectacle he makes in his abject slavery to it!

Crutches for by and by—yes, that is just what our bad habits are. Do we realize how surely and tyrannously they make moral as well as physical cripples of us?   —*Zion's Herald.*

TEN WAYS TO HELP MOTHER

1. Look pleasant.
2. Speak softly and kindly.
3. Do your work cheerfully and well.
4. Do not wait to be told every little duty, but surprize her by doing things she has not told you to do.
5. See how many times you can save her steps by running errands.
6. Put your cap, coat, and school-books in their proper places. Then you will not need to trouble her to help you find them, and the home will look more tidy.
7. Let her know that you are thankful for what she does for you.
8. Notice when she is tried, or is not feeling well, or has a headache, and be quiet.
9. Say to her sometimes, "I love you."
10. Pray for her.

If you follow these suggestions, there will be at least two happy persons—you and your mother. Try it and see.

YOU WILL NEVER BE SORRY

FOR bridling your tongue when about to say something you should not say.

For thinking the best possible of the doings of others.

For forgiving those who have wronged you.

For having given money to mission work.

For being prompt in keeping your promises.
For being patient with stubborn playmates.
For speaking a kind word to a poor, sad child.
For sympathizing with the oppressed.
For shedding forth a good influence.
For asking pardon when in the wrong.
For refusing to listen to vulgar stories.
For being honest in everything.
For harboring clean thoughts.
For thinking before speaking.
For honoring your parents.
For having a sunny spirit.
For being courteous.

"THE BOY FOR ME"

A GENTLEMAN advertised for a boy, and nearly fifty came to see him. Out of the whole number he chose one, and dismissed the rest.

"I should like to know," said a friend, "why you picked out that boy, who has not a single recommendation."

"You are mistaken," said the gentleman; "he had a great many. He wiped his feet when he came in, and closed the door after him, showing that he was careful.

"He gave his seat instantly to that lame old man, showing that he was thoughtful and kind. He took off his cap and answered my questions promptly, showing that he was gentlemanly.

"He picked up the book which I had purposely laid on the floor, and replaced it upon the table; and he waited quietly for his turn, instead of pushing and crowding, showing that he was honorable and orderly.

"When I talked to him I noticed that his clothes were brushed, and his hair in order; when he wrote his name I noticed that his finger-nails were clean.

"Don't you call those little things recommendations? I do; and I would give more for what I can tell about a boy by using my eyes than for all the letters he can bring."   —*Selected*.

MOTHER KNOWS

Nobody knows of the work it makes
   To keep the house together,
Nobody knows of the steps it takes—
   Nobody knows but mother.
Nobody listens to childish woes,
   Which kisses only smother;
Nobody's pained by the naughty blows—
   Nobody, only mother.

Nobody knows of the sleepless care
   Bestowed on baby brother,
Nobody knows of the tender prayer—
   Nobody knows but mother.
Nobody knows of lessons taught
   Of loving one another,
Nobody knows of the patience sought—
   Nobody, only mother.

Nobody knows the anxious fears
   Lest darlings may not weather
Storms of life in coming years—
   Nobody knows but mother.
Nobody knows of the tears that start,
   The grief she gladly smothers;
Nobody knows of the breaking heart—
   Nobody, only mother.

Nobody clings to the wayward child,
   Though scorned by every other,
Leads it so gently from pathways wild—
   Nobody can but mother.
Nobody knows of the hourly prayer
   For him, our erring brother,
Pride of her heart, so pure and fair—
   Nobody, only mother.

—Selected.

THE SNOWBALL

I WONDER if these three boys with their sister have been throwing snowballs until they have become tired and are now going to see how large a snowball they can make. They certainly are having a good time. One boy is waving his cap in the air. Two other boys are coming to join in the sport. One is running as fast as he can with both hands up ready to help roll the snowball; the other boy is climbing over the fence.

When they get the ball so large that they can not roll it, perhaps they will make a snowman out of it. I think most children think it is

fun to make snowmen and throw snowballs, but they sometimes get into trouble when doing so. Some boy may get hurt; he then gets angry and fights the boy who threw the snowball; then their fun is all spoiled. We should not get angry if we get hurt when playing, but should remember the one who hurt us did not mean to do so.

I once read of a boy who threw a snowball through a man's window. This boy's name was George. What do you think George did? Do you think he ran away so the man would not know who broke the window? No; he went to the man and confessed that he had broken the window and said that he was very sorry. George had a new silver dollar that some one had given him for Christmas. He gave it to the man to pay for the broken window.

The man saw George's father and told him that George had broken the window and had given him the dollar to pay for it. He gave the dollar back to George's father. The father was so pleased to know his boy had been honest and truthful that he not only returned to him the dollar he had given the man to pay for the broken window, but also gave him another dollar.

Some time after this the man whose window George had broken wanted a boy to stay in his store, so he sent for George. Do you know why he wanted George? It was because he knew he was an honest boy. When he broke the man's window he told the truth about it.

It is always best to tell the truth. No doubt, this boy felt sorry to give up the new silver dollar that had been given him for Christmas, but he knew it was right for him to pay for the window he had broken, and by doing so he had a chance to earn much more money.

Boys should always be honest and truthful. —*Flossie E. Nisley.*

HOW MUCH DO YOU OWE?

A LAD named Sydney, who had reached the age of ten, overheard a conversation about certain bills which had to be paid, and conceived the idea of making out a bill for what he himself had done. The next morning he quietly laid on his mother's plate at breakfast the following statement: "Mother owes Sydney: For getting coal six times, 6d. For fetching logs lots of times, 6d. For going on errands twice, 4d. For being a good boy, 2d. Total, 1s. 6d."

His mother read the bill, but said nothing. That evening Sydney found it lying on his own plate with the 1s. 6d. as payment; but accompanying it was another bill, which read as follows: "Sydney owes Mother: For his happy home for ten years, nothing. For being good to him, nothing. Total, nothing."

When the lad had looked at this, his eyes were dim and his lips quivering. Presently he took the 1s. 6d. out of his pocket, and rushed to his mother, flung his arms around her neck and exclaimed, "Mother, dear! I was a mean wretch! Please forgive me, and let me do lots of things for you still."   —*Bits for Our Boys.*

WHAT BECAME OF A LIE

First somebody told it,
Then the room wouldn't hold it,
So the busy tongues rolled it
   Till they got it outside,
When the crowd came across it
And never once lost it,
But tossed it and tossed it
   Till it grew long and wide.

From a very small lie, sir,
It grew deep and high, sir,
Till it reached to the sky, sir,
   And frightened the moon;
For she hid her sweet face, sir,
In a veil of cloud-lace, sir,
At the dreadful disgrace, sir,
   That happened at noon.

This lie brought forth others,
Dark sisters and brothers,
And fathers and mothers—
   A terrible crew;
And while headlong they hurried,
The people they flurried,
And troubled and worried,
   As lies always do.

And so, evil-bodied,
This monster lie goaded,
Till at last it exploded
   In smoke and in shame;
When from mud and from mire
The pieces flew higher,
And hit the sad liar
   And killed his good name!

                              —*Mrs. M. A. Kidder.*

THE SPIDER'S WEB

HAVE you ever seen a fly get into a spider's web? When he is once caught he can never get out again. All over the web is a sticky glue which holds him fast. As soon as the spider knows that a fly is caught he comes and kills it.

Satan has a web that is worse than the spider's web. It is the saloon web. In it he catches men and women, sometimes even boys and girls. The spider that does the killing is strong drink. This web does not hold the prisoner fast at once, but when the first drink is taken, the second is wanted, then the third, and so on till at last strong drink robs its victim of many things that are most precious. It takes his strength, his mind, his love, and his home. The Bible says that no drunkard shall inherit the kingdom of heaven. "Wine is a mocker, strong drink is raging, and whosoever is deceived thereby is not wise."

The spider's web looked pretty to the fly, but it deceived him, for it was a trap. Some young boys think it looks manly to drink, but it is only one of Satan's traps to deceive people. Boys and girls, be careful, and you can keep out of Satan's spider-web.

—*Mrs. B. Blackwell.*

EXCLUSIVE FRIENDSHIPS

THERE are some friendships which glory in being exclusive. Take the case of Milly and Mary, for instance. As their affections for each other grew, it seemed to crowd out other affections. Milly was a little jealous of the girls who had been especially intimate with Mary before her own intimacy began, and Mary had the same feeling toward Milly's old friends. The result was that they saw less and less of other girls and more and more of each other. They walked to and from school together. At recess they were always to be seen with their arms about each other's waist. Neither liked to accept an invitation which did not include the other.

If they were separated during vacation, as sometimes happened, they wrote to each other daily, and no matter how good a time they might be having, openly rejoiced to have it end, that they might be together again.

These intimate and exclusive friendships are very likely to appeal to the imagination of young girls, but there is a great deal to be said

against them. The best friend for you is not the girl who has no eyes
for any one but you, but the one who has many friends and love enough
to go around. The affection which shuts out all but the two most con-
cerned is too selfish to be desirable. No girl can restrict her friendship
to a single person without narrowing herself. It is as big a mistake as
to read only one book or to eat only one kind of food.

These intense friendships are very likely to come to a sudden
and violent end. They break down by their own weight. They exact
too much to be enduring. Sooner or later something happens, and the
breaking off of such friendships generally means that hostility takes
the place of the overardent affection.

Don't restrict yourself to one friend, however charming she may
be. Don't let yourself feel that you can't be happy anywhere without
her. You may prefer roses to violets or lilies-of-the-valley, but that is
no good reason for weeding the latter plants out of your garden. The
sensible way is to enjoy the fragrance of all sweet flowers and the
friendship of all sweet girls.   —*Girl's Companion.*

THE GIRLS THAT ARE WANTED

The girls that are wanted are home girls—
  Girls that are mother's right hand,
That fathers and brothers can trust in,
  And the little ones understand.

Girls that are fair on the hearthstone,
  And pleasant when nobody sees;
Kind and sweet to their own folk,
  Ready and anxious to please.

Girls that are wanted are wise girls,
  That know what to do and to say;
That drive with a smile or a soft word
  The wrath of the household away.

The girls that are wanted are good girls—
  Good from the heart to the lips;
Pure as the lily is white and pure
  From its heart to its sweet leaf-tips.

                            —*Selected.*

"IF I HAD THIS OR THAT—"

When Abraham Lincoln was a lad
  And lived in a hut in the wood,
No books, no lamp, no time he had,
  And yet it is understood
He trudged many miles to borrow a book;
The light of the flickering fire he took
  And studied whenever he could;
And none of his friends ever heard him say,
In a self-excusing and hopeless way,
  "If I had this or that I would."

When Joan of Arc was a little maid,
  Untutored, gentle, good,
And France was conquered and dismayed
  By England's masterhood,
She had no wealth nor armament;
Alone with her faith the little maid went
  And freed her land as she could;
And nobody ever heard her say,
In a listless, longing, empty way,
  "If I had this or that I would."

When young James Watt sat by the fire
  And watched the burning wood,
He saw the kettle's lid mount higher,
  Observed and understood;
He had no need of a laboratory
To plan his great steam-engine's glory;
  He used his eye as he could,
And he never once was heard to say,
In a shiftless, thriftless, futile way,
  "If I had this or that I would."

If now you will read your histories o'er
  (As I earnestly think you should)
The fact will impress you more and more
  In the lives of the great and good,
That they were those who never held back
For circumstance or material lack,
  But arose and did what they could;
And never a one was heard to say,
In a weak, surrendering, doubting way,
  "If I had this or that I would."

                    —*Stella George Stern Perry, in St. Nicholas.*

2011

"I'M LITTLE, BUT I'LL TRY"

HERE is a story which the press dispatches carried last winter, and it is worth while for every boy and girl to read it and to apply the remark of little Eileen Martin to the plain work of a plain, every-day life.

Eileen Martin is the daughter of a section foreman on a great railroad line. She lives in Alta, California, and near her home the Overland Limited flashes past on its journey between the East and the West. Though she is a girl, she loves to watch the railroad trains go by as well as any boy does.

One day she had gone to the track to watch the Overland Limited whirl past, and while she was waiting, her quick eye noted a broken rail. She is only seven years old, but she knew that when the swift-flying train struck the rail, destruction and death would result. She also knew the semaphore signals. She knew that when the long arm on the high pole dropped, pointing downward, a train had entered a given space, called a block.

When Eileen saw the broken rail, she at once ran to the telephone and called the station-agent nearest her, and told of the disaster await-ing the train. In an instant's glance at the clock he saw that he could not reach it in time to save it.

"Can't you flag it?" he shouted to the little girl standing on a stool and listening at the other end of his line.

"I'm pretty little, but I'll try," answered Eileen. She quickly called an older sister, and they two ran together down the track. The long arm of the semaphore had dropped. The time was short, and death was near. Yet on they ran, waving their aprons, desperately trying to stop the train. And they did stop it. The engineer saw them and with instant and quick action brought the long, heavy train to a standstill.

Now, this story is worth reading because it is the account of an heroic act. It is worth reading for other reasons.

"I'm pretty little, but I'll try." This is what makes it worth reading. Eileen was little, "pretty little," but she was alert. Her quick eye saw the rail and the dropped semaphore. Her mind was not stupid, else she would not have known what these signs meant. She had listened when others talked of them; she had doubtless asked when there was no other way to find out. Her mind must have been

Semaphore - Signal Light

always wide awake to observe things, to wonder what they meant, and to find out, if possible.

Here was something wrong. It must be told, and told without delay. She could not run and ask mother or father or teacher. What was done, she must do at once. She was "pretty little," but she knew what a telephone could do. She knew that by its aid her voice could outrun the fastest horse—even the fast-flying train, bearing down to destruction. She decided instantly what to do, and did it.

Then came the hardest strain of all. Past the agent the train had flashed. She alone could save it, if anybody could. "Can't you stop it?" came the demand over the wire; and without one moment's hesitation, she replied, "I'll try."

It was the best she could do—little seven-year-old. But how nobly she succeeded! And the qualities that made her success are worthy of consideration by every one. "I'll try!" "I'll try!" that spirit will accomplish things when every other fails.

No matter how young, how little, how weak you are, there is always something for you to do; and Eileen's words are a grand motto: "I'm pretty little, but I'll try."   —*Unidentified*.

A BIRD FOR A BOARDER

MOST birds have no regular boarding-place, but must hunt for their food till they find it. Of course, the old birds find feed and bring it to the young ones till they are large enough to hunt it for themselves, but after that each one must search for its own meal or go hungry. If a bird becomes lazy and does not hunt its dinner, it has to go hungry. Don't you think that would cure it of laziness? If some boys and girls could eat only when they were willing to work, they too would have to go hungry, for some do not like to work and will not if they can help it. Did you know the Bible said that "if any would not work, neither should they eat"? You may find this in 2 Thess. 3:10. God does not want people, even boys and girls, to be lazy. Only those who are willing to do what they can, will ever amount to much in this world or can please the Lord.

But you say that this is not telling about the bird boarder. Well, all right; so it isn't, but it is a lesson that all need to know. Now here's the story. Once upon a time—you know that is the way stories usually begin—once upon a time we lived out in the country near a large woods which was full of birds and squirrels. It was in the summer-time, and the door was open. As we were eating supper one evening a little bird came hopping in at the open door and began looking for something to eat. We carefully threw a few crumbs out toward it and kept very still. Soon it began to eat them, and so we threw down some more. It ate all it wanted, looked around a while and flew away.

We were pleased, of course, to have such a visitor, but we did not expect ever to see it again. The very next evening, however, when we were at supper, here it came again. It kept on coming, hardly ever missing a day, for a long time. It grew so tame that it would fly to us out in the yard and hop around our feet just out of reach, and would eat the crumbs that we gave it.

But at last a sad ending came. One evening when it came for its supper, an old cat sitting in the yard saw the little bird, pounced upon it, and ran off with it; and we never saw our little bird boarder any more. Of course, we were all very sorry, for we had come to think a great deal of it.   —*C. W. Naylor.*

REAPING WHAT HE HAD SOWN

IN OUR every-day life we meet with a great many people in various pitiful conditions, many having brought these sad conditions upon themselves by disobeying the laws of nature and of God. Some time ago, while in the post-office building of one of our cities, I chanced to meet a man who for twenty years had been a cigaret-fiend. He was in a very pitiful condition. His bodily strength was almost gone, his mind was weakened, and his poor soul was in despair.

Prompted by some motive, he began telling about his past life. At the youthful age of fourteen years he began to smoke the poisonous cigaret, and he had continued to do so until a few weeks before, when, on account of his awful condition, he was compelled to quit the habit.

When he began smoking he perhaps thought it manly to do so, but alas! too late he sees his mistake. Now, at a comparatively young age, just what should be the bloom of life, his health is gone and he is near death's door. He has begun to reap what he has sown.

So it is in all things. Whatsoever we sow we shall also reap. We need only to look around us to see that this is true. When we see the misery and suffering of people brought on by their engaging in sinful practises, we are made to think of the words of the apostle Paul in Gal. 6:7, 8: "Be not deceived; God is not mocked: for whatsoever a man soweth, that shall he also reap. For he that soweth to his flesh, shall of the flesh reap corruption; but he that soweth to the Spirit, shall of the Spirit reap life everlasting."

Not only shall we reap in eternity, but also we may partly reap the harvest in this life. This poor man is reaping in this life a part of what he has sown.

We should be very careful about the kind of seed we are sowing. If we sow bad seed we must reap suffering, disease to our bodies, poverty, and disagreeable things in this life, and in the life to come eternal banishment from God. If we sow good seed we shall reap joy, happiness, peace, and all that is good in this life, and a home in heaven in the life to come. Therefore, dear reader, be careful what kind of seed you sow.   —*Earl L. Martin.*

WHAT A BOY CAN DO

THERE are some things a Christian boy can do who wants to work for Jesus:

Be frank.
Be polite.
Be obliging.
Obey his parents.
Keep himself tidy.
Refuse to do wrong.
Never use profanity.
Never learn to smoke.
Be useful about home.
Keep out of bad company.
Never laugh at a coarse joke.
Learn his lessons thoroughly.
Never make unnecessary noise.
Never be disrespectful to old age.
Be kind to his brothers and sisters.
Take the part of those who are ill-used.

Never make fun of another because he is poor.

Never play marbles for "keeps"; it is gambling.

Fail, if he can not pass his examination honestly.

Never tell or listen to a story which he would not repeat to his mother.

WHAT IS YOUR MOTTO?

WHEN I went into an office one day I saw placed upon a desk a pretty little motto, which the worker said he was trying to live up to every day. This motto was on the desk, but some people carry their mottos around on themselves, so that everybody can see what they are trying to live up to every day. These mottos are not printed, but they are written in a much plainer and surer way, so there can be no mistaking their meaning.

Jim goes yelling by with a look of mischief in his eyes. The cat runs under something to hide, his little sister begins to gather up her dolls and to look worried, and even the dog looks as if he felt uneasy. Now, anybody can tell that Jim's motto is, "It is fun to tease."

Harry goes to school with his hair uncombed and his hands and face dirty; he walks with a careless, shuffling gait, and often he is late at school; he does not run and play much, as the other boys do, but likes to sit down and stretch and yawn. Who would have to guess to know that his motto is, "Be lazy"?

Claude is a contrary boy. He will not mind anybody if he can help it. He will say his motto to his mother if she asks him to carry in wood, and he says it to the boys at school if they want him to do anything. He keeps saying it all the time, and yet if you would ask him what his life motto is, maybe he would not be able to tell you. Here it is: "I don't have to."

Fannie wants a new dress; so she coaxes and whines till her mother promises to get it for her. She wants to visit one of the other girls, but Mama thinks it not best; but Fannie begins to cry and beg, and keeps it up till Mama does let her go for a little while. Her face is all ready to pucker up if she can not have her way. Now it is plain that her motto is, "Coax and whine till you get what you want."

Alice is nearly always dressed prettily. She twists round so proudly showing off her new dresses that she makes poor little Kate feel that she is not fit to be with her because she can not have fine dresses too. When she talks to the other girls it is mostly about her new clothes or her beautiful hat, or about how she was dressed when she went to meeting or somewhere else. Her motto is "Dress up."

Grace is at home washing dishes and singing as she works. When she has finished the dishes, she will sweep and dust. She improves every opportunity to help Mother and is a great comfort to her. She is willing to hurry home from school each evening so as to do her share of the work. Now, her motto is as easy to read as can be: "Be Mother's helper."

Will stopped to open the door for Mother; he picked up a book that Grandmother had dropped; he smiled and spoke to an old lady on the street; he took off his hat as he went into the house; and he rose and offered his chair to an old man who came in. Now, is it not plain that his motto is, "Be polite"?

Lottie does not run to the door and stare at the man her father is talking with; she will not break into a conversation with some of her questions, but waits till she can speak without interrupting; she sits up straight at the table, and does not cram her mouth too full nor laugh too loud; if she has to walk in front of any one, she always says, "Excuse me." Her motto surely is, "Have good manners."

Jessie gave the best apple to May, and when she went out with her to swing she let May swing first. When there was a chance for one of the children to go for a ride, she let her little brother go and she stayed at home. She takes the smallest piece of cake, or if there is only a little of anything, she goes without rather than to rob another. Her motto is, "Be unselfish."

Merton took the finest peach, and he wore the new glove all the morning when the boys were playing ball. When he saw Uncle Frank drive up in his car, he thought he might get a ride; so he ran off and left little Rollo crying because he could not keep up. He took his choice first of the presents that Grandma had brought. Of course, his motto is, "I look out for myself."

Lettie laid her book down and helped Fred mend his kite. She tied up Nellie's cut finger. She carried some flowers to a sick child. She wanted very much to go and spend the afternoon with Bertha, but as the baby was so cross she stayed and helped Mother instead.

Every day she proves to us that her motto is, "Be kind and thoughtful."
    Now, these folks do not have their mottos written with letters on their backs, yet everybody reads them. They tell their mottos by their actions. We always show by our actions what our real self is.

                                    —*Mabel Hale.*

DON'T FORGET YOUR DAD

A friend is a precious fortune
    In this world of hearts and love;
A sister is man's great blessing—
    A guide to the realm above;
The companionship of a brother
    Helps to keep away life's care;
But there's one who, when you need him,
    Never fails to do his share.

Playmates, sweethearts, chums, and lovers
    Bring their joys to the heart;
But they each bring hours of sorrow
    When the time has come to part;
And when all of them have drifted
    Far away on life's wide sea,
There is still one who will comfort
    You with love and sympathy.

Mother—oh, sweet, gentle mother!
    As I write these lines, I pray
That no mind may misconstrue them,
    And that lips may never say
I would take one single leaflet
    From the love-wreath that she wears;
For my own heart adds a portion
    To a love the whole world shares.

But there's one who toils unceasing
    For his loved ones and his home,
While the storms of life oppress him,
    When life's sea is lashed to foam.
I would offer up a tribute—
    But I'm just an humble lad—
So I'll end by simply saying,
    Don't forget your dear old dad.

                                    —*Charles H. Meiers.*

RULES FOR USING BOOKS

GOOD books are treasures and should be handled with the greatest of care by every one. Here are a few rules that every boy and girl should observe in using books:

Never hold a book near a fire.

Never drop a book upon the floor.

Never turn leaves with the thumb.

Never lean or rest upon an open book.

Never turn down the corners of leaves.

Never touch a book with damp or soiled hands.

Always place a large book upon a table before opening it.

Never pull a book from the shelf by the binding at the top but by the back.

Never close a book with a pencil, tablet, or anything else bulky, between the leaves.

Never lend a borrowed book, but return it as soon as you are done with it.

Always keep a borrowed book covered with paper while it is in your possession.   —*Selected.*

PLAY FAIR

THE boys were playing hide-and-seek, and it was Tom's time to hide his eyes. He did so; but when all the boys were busy trying to find a good place to hide, he peeped and saw where John hid and soon patted for him. John thought Tom peeped, but was not sure. Afterward, while they were playing ball, Tom broke some of the rules so that he could win. The boys were angry, but he just laughed.

Tom was a fine fellow in many ways, always good-natured and full of fun, but every time he could he would cheat in playing games. It was the same way with his lessons. If he could look over some one's shoulder into his book, he would do so. He would not study hard and get his lessons well, but depended on cheating to make his grades. He went through all his school-days this way and thought himself smarter than the boys who dug things out for themselves. He would even laugh at the other boys for studying so hard when they could get along so easy.

Tom is a man now—and such a man! I know you do not want to be like him. They say he will cheat his best friend if he gets a chance. He is known as a dishonest man, one who must be watched all the time. He does not pay his debts unless he is brought before the law, and he will tell an untruth to make even a little trade. Poor Tom! One of these days he will have to stand before God, and there he can not deceive. What will he do then?

You would not be such a man as Tom is, but he began his downward course by not playing fair at school. Do not be like him. Play fair.   —*Mabel Hale.*

A BOY'S PROMISE

The school was out, and down the street
  A noisy crowd came thronging,
The hue of health and gladness sweet
  To every face belonging.

Among them strode a little lad,
  Who listened to another,
And mildly said, half grave, half sad,
  "I can't—I promised mother."

A shout went up, a ringing shout
  Of boisterous derision;
But not one moment left in doubt
  That manly, brave decision.

"Go where you please, do what you will,"
  He calmly told the other;
"But I shall keep my word, boys, still;
  I can't—I promised mother."

Ah! who could doubt the future course
  Of one who thus had spoken?
Through manhood's struggle, gain and loss,
  Could faith like this be broken?

God's blessing on that stedfast will,
  Unyielding to another,
That bars all jeers and laughter still,
  Because he promised mother.
                       —*Selected.*

A LESSON FROM THE BUFFALO

THE buffalo is an animal very much like cattle in both appearance and habits, but considerably larger. In kindness to him the Creator has favored him in many respects above most other wild animals.

In the first place, the buffalo has great strength. He can run for many hours without becoming fatigued. This is very useful in escaping from his enemies and from prairie fires. It is also a great advantage in fighting what few enemies he has.

As his home was principally in the central part of the United States and Canada, he found his long, soft coat of hair a great protection against the bitter cold and blizzards of winter. Especially was this true when his home happened to be in the far north.

He was well armed with large pointed horns. They were very much like those of an ox, but shorter and better adapted for his protection. Wielding these with his great strength, he needed to fear but little from wolves, which are the dread of less favored animals, and are about the only foes he had, except man.

If a single buffalo was attacked by a pack of wolves, a number of the strongest and boldest of his mates immediately rushed to his assistance. Before the blows from their fine horns, the enemies were soon put to flight.

But if a buffalo was discovered to be in a feeble condition, a pack of these sneaking enemies would follow him for days. At a moment when he was unaware and had neglected to keep himself in safe quarters among his mates, they would pounce upon him and overcome him. But he did not give in at the first attack. Bold and defiant while life remained, he fought to the last, and not until they were already tearing the very flesh from his bones would he give up the unequal struggle.

In the ways in which the buffalo protected himself against insects he showed a kind of brute wisdom. He would choose any large stone to be found on the plains, and would rub himself on this to get rid of the pests. He used these stones so much that around almost every large stone on the prairies there is still to be seen a large hole in the ground. These holes are sometimes six feet deep, worn by his hoofs and the action of the wind. These stones are known to the settlers as "rubbing-stones." It was also his habit to wallow in the mud, and thus cover himself with a protection against insects. He was fond of going in herds. This also was a safeguard against his enemies.

As the buffalo was so strong and vigorous and so well protected against the elements and his foes, it would be natural to think that buffaloes would have become very numerous. This was the case. Indeed, we can hardly realize the vast numbers that once roamed over the prairies. We are told that single herds containing millions of these animals have been seen to blacken the plains as far as the eye could reach. These immense herds sometimes even stopped railway trains.

But what has become of these creatures? and why do we not see some of them now? They have been slaughtered by the use of the rifle, only a few being kept in parks, shows, etc.

True, they have left their marks on the country, for all over the plains that they inhabited, and that have not been plowed by the white man, may still be seen a complete network of trails. These were worn deep by their hoofs as they went to and fro to get their food and water. Now as the footman crosses these prairies he comes very often upon a little pile of white bones. As he sees them he realizes that this is all that remains of one of a species of beasts that once held almost complete sway over this vast country, and were nearly as numerous as the stars of the sky.

But they themselves are to blame to a great extent for the fact that they were destroyed so fast. They were very careless in the midst of greatest danger. When another animal would have quickly fled to a place of safety the buffalo would stand with the greatest unconcern and watch his comrades slaughtered one by one, until he himself should suffer the same fate. Without seeing or seeming to see any danger whatever, he would walk directly into a quicksand or quagmire in which he could see his fellows already struggling for life. He was so stubborn, also, that it was almost impossible to turn him from his course when once he had made up his mind.

Thus, we see that although God had endowed them with a strong body, an excellent coat of hair for protection, armed them with two fine horns, and had given them plenty of broad fields over which to roam; yet because of their carelessness, their failing to watch, and their stubbornness, they have been easily reduced to a very few in number.

Among men these three faults have ruined many an otherwise promising life. "He that trusteth in his own heart is a fool: but whoso walketh wisely, he shall be delivered" (Prov. 28:26).

—W. Robert Hines.

BOYS WE LIKE

THE boy who never makes fun of old age, no matter how decrepit or unfortunate or evil it may be. God's hand rests lovingly on the aged head.

The boy who never cheats or is unfair in his play. Cheating is contemptible anywhere and at any age. His play should strengthen, not weaken his character.

The boy who never calls anybody bad names, no matter what anybody calls him.

The boy who is never cruel.

The boy who never lies. Even white lies leave black spots on the character.

The boy who never makes fun of a companion because of a misfortune he could not help.

The boy who never hesitates to say "No" when asked to do a wrong thing.

The boy who never quarrels.

The boy who never forgets that God made him to be a joyous, loving, helpful being.   —*Philadelphia Public Ledger.*

IF I ONLY HAD A CHANCE

MANY a boy dreams of the great things he would do if he only "had a chance." A dozen homely duties are crowding about him, but he wants a chance to show that he is of different stuff from ordinary boys; and so he dreams and chafes at his commonplace surroundings until his opportunities are gone, and then he takes up the wail of, "If I had only had a chance."

The boys who succeed in life are the boys who make their own chances, or who see in every little thing about them a chance for faithful, conscientious work. Are you poor? Poverty is a stern teacher, but her lessons have been prized by many great men who have passed through her school. Have you no influential friend to help you along? Turner, the painter, was a barber's son; Prideaux, the scholar and theologian, scoured pots and pans while working his way through college. Sir Isaac Newton, the greatest astronomer of his time, once peddled cabbage on the streets. Martin Luther, when a boy at school, sang in the streets for the pence which passers-by might give him. The late Judge Bradley, of the United States Supreme Court, was the son of a charcoal-burner.

There is more in the boy than the chance. A thousand chances may pass unheeded by a careless, unobservant lad, whereas the boy with the right sort of stuff in him would seize the first one. Patience, faithfulness, truthfulness, and downright honesty count for more than chances.   —*Selected.*

THE FOUR PLANTS

AN OLD teacher was once taking a walk through a forest with a pupil by his side. The old man suddenly stopped and pointed to four plants close at hand. The first was just beginning to peep above the ground, the second had rooted itself pretty well into the earth, the third was a small shrub, while the fourth and last was a full-sized tree. The tutor said to his young companion:

"Pull up the first."

The boy easily pulled it up with his fingers.

"Now pull up the second."

The youth obeyed, but found the task not so easy.

"And now the third."

The boy had to put forth all his strength and use both arms before he succeeded in uprooting it.

"And now," said the master, "try your hand upon the fourth."

But lo! when the youth grasped the trunk of the tall tree in his arms, he could hardly move it enough to shake the leaves.

"This, my son, is just what happens with our bad habits. When they are young we can cast them out readily, but only divine power can uproot them when they are old."   —*Exchange.*

FIVE RESOLUTIONS

JONATHAN Edwards, who left a greater mark upon America than almost any other man among her earlier thinkers, made five resolutions for himself in his youth and lived by them faithfully. To study them is to see one secret of his greatness. To adopt them will make any young person nearer to greatness himself. They are as follows:

1. Resolved: To live with all my might while I do live.

2. Resolved: Never to lose one moment of time, but to improve it in the most profitable way I possibly can.

3. Resolved: Never to do anything which I should despise or think meanly of in another.

4. Resolved: Never to do anything out of revenge.

5. Resolved: Never to do anything which I should be afraid to do if it were the last hour of my life.

These resolutions did not come from a weak nature nor from a character free from temptation and faults. They prove that by internal evidence. . . . These are the resolves of a striving young soul, conscious of its own dangers and weaknesses. That is their value and their inspiration. To adopt them is to take up the same struggle, and through it to win nobility, virtue, and elevation of character just as Jonathan Edwards did long ago. *—Selected.*

RETURN THE BOOK

HAVE you a book borrowed from a friend? Then be prompt to return it when you have finished using it. How few people there are who are careful to return a book lent them! And yet each one expects what he lends to be returned.

Most people prize their books and enjoy sharing the contents of a good book with their friends, but they expect it to be thoughtfully cared for, and returned at the proper time. It is embarrassing to have to ask for the return of anything lent; yet the constant neglect, forgetfulness, or carelessness of those who borrow often makes this unpleasant task necessary.

It is very convenient to borrow sometimes, and we should show our appreciation of the lender's favor by promptly returning any borrowed article when we have finished using it. Kindness and courtesy demand this of us. Let us cultivate this excellent habit.

THE TEST OF EDUCATION

A PROFESSOR in the University of Chicago told his pupils that he should consider them educated, in the best sense of the word, when they could say yes to every one of fourteen questions he should put to them. Here are the questions:

Has your education given you sympathy with all good causes and made you espouse them?

Has it made you public-spirited?

Has it made you a brother to the weak?

Have you learned how to make friends and keep them?

Do you know what it is to be a friend yourself?

Can you look an honest man or a pure woman straight in the eye?

Do you see anything to love in a little child?

Will a lonely dog follow you in the street?

Can you be high-minded and happy in the meaner drudgeries of life?

Do you think washing dishes and hoeing corn just as compatible with high thinking as piano-playing or golf?

Are you good for anything to yourself? Can you be happy, alone?

Can you look out on the world and see anything except dollars and cents?

Can you look into a mud puddle by the wayside and see anything in the puddle but mud?

Can you look into the sky at night and see beyond the stars? Can your soul claim relationship with the Creator? —*Selected.*

SOME REASONS FOR FAILURE

THERE is no success for the young man—
  Who vacillates.
Who is faint-hearted.
Who shirks responsibility.
Who never dares to take risks.
Who thinks fate is against him.
Who is discouraged by reverses.
Who does not believe in himself.
Who expects nothing but failure.
Who is always belittling himself.
Who is always anticipating trouble.
Who waits for something to turn up.
Who complains that he never had a chance.
Who is constantly grumbling about his work.
Who never puts his heart into anything he does.
Who blames circumstances or other people for his failures.
Who can do a poor day's work without a protest from his conscience.
Who assumes the attitude of a victim whom everybody is bent on "doing."
Who expects to eliminate from his work everything that is disagreeable or distasteful.
Who is forever wishing that he were doing something else instead of the thing he is doing.
Who clings tenaciously to old ideas and old ways of doing things and is a slave of precedent. —*Selected.*

CAN AND CAN'T

Can and Can't once ran a race.
Can fell down and hurt his face,
But up he jumped and on he ran,
The persevering little man.
In spite of all Can't did or said,
Can kept on going straight ahead.
Can't did not wish to be the last,
Nor did he like to run so fast,
And so he shouted, "Don't you see
That you can never outrun me?"
But Can replied, "That's just your way.
You're telling people every day
They can't do this and can't do that,
That black is white, the earth is flat;
But you'll not conquer me, for I
Intend to win this race or die."
They kept on running many years,
And Can at times shed bitter tears
Over the troubles that he met
And oftentimes would weary get.
His feet were sore, the way was rough,
The road did not seem short enough.
He sometimes ran and sometimes hopped,
But never, never, never stopped.
At last Can't halted by the way,
And said, "Now I will rest and play."
And so he waited while his friend
Kept on until he reached the end.
And Can't was left far in the rear
Because he wou'd not persevere.
Can won the race while Can't stood still;
He always has, and always will.

—*Selected.*

PLAYING WITH A SNAKE

THERE was a man among the Florida lagoons who kept a pet rattlesnake in his hallway. He was a learned man, a literary man in a small way, and he had long lived in that hot, sand-strewn land. So had the serpent. In fact, they had lived together, the man in the house and the reptile in the cage, for nearly twenty years.

This man was a tease, and the snake had an irritable temper. Every morning his master, just as he came down to breakfast, would

 stick a finger into the cage to see the hissing, wrathful creature leap at it. For twenty years he kept up the foolish habit. His friends warned him; his wife pleaded with him; not a few scientists who visited him remonstrated. Still every morning he thrust the finger in, and every morning the snake sprang in vain, until one day the poisoned fangs · clipped his finger. That evening he died.

These facts—they are facts —come bitterly home to an observer when he sees a young fellow tempting some sin or vice, playing with it, sticking his soul nearer, nearer to the cage. The young fellow cries: "I'll never be overcome. I can stand a glass of beer. I can keep clean and fool around uncleanliness. I can spend more money than I earn, and yet stay honest." But some morning that young man will wake up and find that the fangs have driven home. Then will the sin he did not run away from bite like a serpent and sting like an adder. Boys, don't keep rattlesnakes in the hallway of your souls.   —*Selected*.

THE VOICE THAT COUNTS

"O FATHER, I wish I could sing! It is so nice to give pleasure to people. Florence sang at the club today, and we all enjoyed it so much. She sings every night to her father, too. I'd give anything if I could, but there's no use wishing. There isn't any music in me."

"Is that so?" asked the father, taking her wistful face between his hands. "Well, perhaps you can't sing. But don't tell me your voice has no music in it. To me it is full of music."

"Why, Father, how can you say so?"

"Almost every evening," answered the father, "when I come home, the first thing is a merry laugh, and it rests me, no matter how tired I am. Yesterday I heard that voice saying, 'Don't cry, Buddie; sister'll mend it for you.' Sometimes I hear it reading to grandmother. Last week I heard it telling Mary: 'I'm sorry your head aches. I'll do the dishes tonight.' That is the kind of music I like best. Don't tell me my little daughter hasn't a sweet voice!"

—Selected.

TRUTHFULNESS REWARDED

I AM GOING to tell you about a boy who was not afraid to tell the truth. This boy was working for a storekeeper. One time the storekeeper had a great many bushels of beans that were damaged. He then bought several bushels of good beans. He went to work and put some of these good beans in the bottoms of barrels and then filled the barrels nearly full of bad beans. At last he put some good beans on top. So no matter what end might be opened good beans would be found. When the beans were all put up in barrels the storekeeper marked them, "Beans A1." When the boy saw the merchant do this he said to him, "Do you think it right, sir, to mark those beans thus?" "It is none of your business," said the merchant in a rough, ugly tone. The boy said no more.

One day a man came into the store and wanted to buy several barrels of beans. Now, a sample of the beans was kept in a box. The man was well pleased with the sample. They were fine beans. He asked the merchant if he could see the beans in the barrels. "Certainly," said the merchant. He then told the boy to go with the gentleman upstairs and open one of the barrels. They went up, and a barrel was opened. The man examined the beans carefully and found them to be just like the sample. He said:

"These are fine beans, and I can not get such beans anywhere else for such a low price."

Then, turning to the boy, he said:

"My young man, are those beans the same quality all the way down."

The boy at first did not know what to say. He knew that the merchant would expect him to say yes; but his conscience told him he ought to say no. He decided to be true, and he said:

"No, sir; they are not."

"Then, I do not want them," said the man, and left. The boy then went down to the office.

"Did you sell that man those beans?" asked the merchant of the boy.

"No, sir," said the boy.

"Why not?" asked the merchant.

"Well, sir, the man asked me if those beans were of such good quality all the way down, and I told him that they were not. Then he said that he did not want them," answered the boy.

The merchant became angry and told the boy to go to the cashier and get his wages, as they did not want such a boy any longer. So he was out of employment. You may think it would have been better for him to tell a lie. Let us see.

Not long afterward this same merchant wanted a boy to fill a very important position. He wanted a boy whom he could fully trust. He remembered this boy and sent for him. He offered him the position at twenty dollars more a month than he was getting before. The boy accepted the position and was thus rewarded in money for his truthfulness. He also had a clear conscience, which was a still greater reward. It pays to tell the truth.   —*Chas. E. Orr.*

A GOOD POTATO OR A GOOD TOMATO

"ONE THING at a time and that well" is a good rule to follow. Every individual should seek to know himself and God's will concerning him. God has a work for every human being to perform. Not all can be ministers or teachers, neither can all be mechanics, farmers, or diplomats; but each person can be some one thing and be efficient in that line of work. It is not best to try to do two things at one time, lest we make a failure.

This thought is beautifully illustrated by Luther Burbank's experiment with the potato and the tomato. Noticing that the leaves on the vines of these two vegetables are very much alike, he proceeded to graft one vine to the other, and the result was a vine on which grew both potatoes and tomatoes. But both vegetables were of an inferior quality. "The tomato was not a good tomato, and the potato was not a good potato."

Seeing this, Mr. Burbank is said to have proceeded to throw the result of his experiment away, deeming it worthless, and probably to have said to the vine before casting it aside:

"I just tried to show you, Mr. Vine, that you can't be two things very successfully. If you're going to be a potato, be a good potato, and don't try to be too many things. It's better to be a great, big, strong, helpful potato than to be a poor little scrawny, half-potato and half tomato. And whatever you do in life after this, Mr. Vine, do that one thing and do it well! Get a job and stick to that one job until you are perfect at it. Don't always be trying to do a lot of things."

—Pina Winters.

SAYINGS OF FRANKLIN

A WORD to the wise is enough.

Sloth, like rust, consumes faster than labor wears; while the used key is always bright.

But dost thou love life? then do not squander time, for that is the stuff life is made of.

If time be of all things the most precious, wasting time must be the greatest prodigality.

Lost time is never found again; and what we call time enough, always proves little enough.

Early to bed, and early to rise, makes a man healthy, wealthy, and wise.

Employ thy time well if thou meanest to gain leisure; and since thou art not sure of a minute, throw not away an hour.

Keep thy shop, and thy shop will keep thee.

Want of care does us more damage than want of knowledge.

A neglect may breed great mischief: for want of a nail the shoe was lost; for want of the shoe the horse was lost; and for want of a horse the rider was lost, being overtaken and slain by the enemy—all for want of a little care about a horseshoe nail.

Fond pride of dress is sure a very curse; ere fancy you consult, consult your purse.

They that will not be counseled, can not be helped.

ONE BLACK SPOT

IT WAS in quiet, country homes in a fair land far away across the deep blue sea, five and seventy years ago, that the two boys of my story were born. Though it was not an angel that gave the name of one of these boys to his parents, yet they always believed that it was God who caused them both to dream the same night, two weeks before the child was born, that they should call him John. The other boy was named Joseph because he was the eleventh son of his parents.

John was born, so records say, fifteen minutes before midnight on May 4, 1843, and Joseph was born fifteen minutes after midnight on May 5, of the same year. John's birthday anniversary was on the fourth of May and Joseph's was on the fifth, yet John drew his first breath of life only thirty minutes before Joseph drew his.

When these boys were five years old their parents, with their families, left the fair land of their nativity to better, if possible, their circumstances in life, in this prosperous western world. It was while on board the gallant ship, crossing the broad Atlantic, that John and Joseph met for the first time. John was short and thick, with broad face, brown eyes, and black hair. Joseph was tall and slender, thin-faced, blue eyed, and light-haired. John was forward, rough, boisterous, quick-tempered, and impulsive. Joseph was reticent, quiet, gentle, mild-tempered, and delicate. Day by day as these boys watched together the splashing of the waves or the occasional passing of another ship, or played together on the deck, they grew rapidly into the affections of each other.

Their parents, with their large families, settled on adjoining farms in the eastern part of the State of Pennsylvania. It was joyous spring-time; the forests were donning their robes of green; the birds were singing in the budding hedge and verdant field; the crows were calling to their fellows as they flew across the broad acres from one stretch of woodland to another; the boys were filled with delight.

During the days of the following summer they were much in the company of each other, wading in the shallow, pebble-bottomed creek, roaming through the fields, and at evening time strolling hand in hand down the long lane to drive the cows home.

The love John and Joseph had for each other grew stronger as the days went by, and the life of the one felt the power of the life of the other, and both were changed. John was not so forward, Joseph was not so backward. John was less boisterous, Joseph was not so quiet. It was noticeable, however, that John was meeting Joseph more than half way.

Two years later, one autumn day found John and Joseph in their first day at school. They sat in the same seat, and when possible were on the same side in the game. But one day it happened that they were on opposite sides. In the close contest the boys were thrown together in the struggle, and they became angered at each other. John dealt Joseph a severe blow in the face. This occurred at the noon-hour. The sad affair was told to the teacher by some of the girls.

When school was called, and all was quiet, the teacher requested the boys to come forward. Then he questioned them concerning their quarrel. Joseph was silent. John told the story, putting as much of the blame on Joseph as he could. He was compelled, however, to confess that he had struck the blow that marked the face of Joseph. The teacher said to John, "I am sorry, but I shall have to punish you." Whereupon, reaching for his whip, he asked John to remove his coat. John made no move. Then Joseph, with big tears in his eyes, began to take off his coat.

"Why are you removing your coat, Joseph? You struck no blow," said the teacher.

"No, I struck no blow," said Joseph, "but I am partly to blame, and I can never endure seeing John bear all the punishment; so please punish me in his stead."

Such devotion won the admiration of the teacher, and after a moment's reflection he let both the boys go unpunished.

That evening as John and Joseph were locked in each other's arms they vowed they would never quarrel again. For these sixty-eight years since that time they have lived neighbors to each other and have faithfully kept their vow. They look back to that boyhood quarrel and call it the one black spot in their long life of love and friendship.

Black spots if treated rightly will make the bright spots brighter. Let us, like these boys, turn the black spots into the cultivation and strengthening of that which is noblest, best, and truest in us.

—*C. E. Orr.*

THE LITTLE BOOTBLACK

N OT LONG ago I read of a noble act of a little boy. A gentleman called for a bootblack to shine his shoes. A little fellow came slowly and placed his box under the gentleman's foot. Before he could get his brush out a larger boy ran up and, gently pushing the little fellow aside, said, "Here, you sit down, Jimmie."

The gentleman, mistaking his motive, sharply told the newcomer to "clear out."

"Oh, that's all right, boss," was the reply. "I'm only going to do it for him. You see he's been sick in the hospital for more than a month and can't do much work yet; so we boys all turn in and give him a lift when we can."

"Is that so, Jimmie?" asked the gentleman, turning to the smaller boy.

"Yes, sir;" wearily replied the boy, "he does it for a time, if you'll let him."

"Certainly, go ahead," said the man; and as the bootblack used his brush the man began questioning him.

"You say all the boys help him in this way?"

"Yes, sir; when they have no job themselves and Jimmie gets one, they turn in and help him, 'cause he ain't very strong yet, you see."

"What part of the money do you keep out for yourself?" was asked.

"I don't keep none; I ain't no such sneak as that," was the reply.

When the shine was completed, the gentleman handed the boy a quarter, saying, "I guess you are a pretty good boy, so you may keep ten cents and give the rest to Jimmie there."

"Can't do it, sir. It's his job. Here, Jim," said the boy, and, throwing him the money, he was off for a job for himself.

How happy this boy must have felt in doing so noble a deed! Jesus says, "It is more blessed to give than to receive." I wonder how many will try to remember this story and practise what this lesson is intended

to teach. Remember, Jesus will bless you if, without a thought for yourself, you will try to help the poor and suffering and show them by your life how Jesus lived.　　　　　　　　　*—Effie Lavell.*

BEGINNING TO BE A MAN

WHILE a boy is a child, he is a part of his father's family. If there be five children, then he is, counting his father and mother, just one seventh of the family, only a fraction. His interests are one with the other members of the family. He thinks and acts and plans for the same purpose and to the same end as father, mother, brothers, and sisters do. He has the same friends and goes to the same places.

After a while he reaches that age when he can no longer be called a child. His interests begin to be different from those of the rest of the family. He wants to work at some special device or plan in which his brothers, sisters, father, and mother are not interested. Possibly he has some new friends that are peculiarly his own and do not, in a way, belong to the rest of the family. He has dreams and notions of his own. His ideals differ from the ideals of those about him. He has some longings, too, with which others are not in sympathy.

All these things show that the boy is beginning to be a man. He is not altogether a man yet, but he is beginning to be one, and there are some things to which he must now adjust himself. A change is always more or less irritating; but when a boy begins to be a man, he is brought face to face with some hard walls to scale. It is good, too, that he has these hard things to encounter; for they, if properly met, strengthen him for the greater things he has to meet later.

As the boy, the fraction, grows into a unit, a separate thing apart, he needs to learn, first of all, to turn to his Creator for wisdom. There are times when he is lonely, for others can not understand him. Often he goes innocently into wrong paths because of his peculiar position. These are times when he needs a friend, and none can exactly fill that place but the Creator. The boy who at this age has learned to turn to God when in need of anything will need few of my words; for he has found a Friend that will crown him with success, happiness, and true manhood.

One of his first hard battles will doubtless be with his own people—father, mother, brothers, sisters—who fail to recognize or to remember about the change that is coming into his life. If he continues to take the place of a little boy, he loses self-respect; but if he contends for the place of a man, troubles of all kinds are likely to arise, and trouble is the one thing he must avoid. Troubles that arise at this time are often the worst troubles there are. At such times the most loving fathers and sons have been separated. Bitterness has sprung up that was worse than death. No boy can afford to lose the confidence and good-will of his father. Every boy needs his father; every father needs his son.

Then, the only thing to be done, if the boy is to be a real man, is to learn how to manage the situation harmoniously. He certainly does not want to have a break with the best friends he has on earth. He needs them, and he knows it. That "uppish," independent spirit that comes along with the stir of manhood he is feeling must be brought under his control just as a trainer brings under control a high-spirited colt. You see, it is going to take a real man-spirit to master the circumstances. Being a real man is a big undertaking, but the person who can get along with his people at home stands a much better chance of reaching the ideal than the one who fails in this, because he has a start in life that has strengthened his moral muscles at the most critical time.

One of the most essential things for a boy to remember at this serious age is his manners. Being polite will tide him over some of the most trying seasons. Always to give an attentive ear when Father speaks and always to reply in a civil way whether or not it is expedient to do what he says, will form a habit that will avoid many a crash when Father is tried and weary with his many cares. Another fine thing for boys at this age to do is to study the disposition of their father and their most trying brother or sister. Learn how to approach them in a way that will not irritate them.

Be careful, also, to show respect for the feelings of others. Boys have a right to their opinions, but the proper kind of boy will never try to make his opinions binding on other people. If they are not received as they should be, show fortitude like a general. Avoid fault-finding. Such a habit shows a weak nature. All parents have faults, but maybe some time they will want to acknowledge them, and it will be a help to them to know that their boy has been a dear enough friend to them to keep their faults to himself. A gentlemanly boy will not contradict or dispute with his father or mother. I turned to look at a certain young man on the street when I was told he treated his parents in a princely manner. He was little and very ordinary in appearance, but I wish I could tell you how I honored him. He was a gentleman. There was no sham there. He was genuine.

Boys, be loyal to those parents who have helped you fight life's battles. You do not know what this has meant to them; the nights and days of toil you can never hope to repay. This is not going to be an easy thing to do, but what does a man amount to until he has learned

how to do some hard things? Solve the home problems, and you will
have little to fear when the great things of life come.

—Mabel C. Porter.

A LAND UNKNOWN

Have you heard the tale of Lazy-lad,
  Who dearly loved to shirk,
For he "hated" his lessons and "hated" his tasks,
  And he "hated" to have to work?
So he sailed away on a summer day
  Over the ocean blue;
Said Lazy-lad, "I will seek till I find
  The land of Nothing-to-do."

So Lazy-lad he sailed to the west,
  And then to the east sailed he,
And he sailed north and he sailed south
  Over many a league of sea.
And many a country fair and bright
  And busy came into view;
But never, alas! could he find the coast
  Of the land of Nothing-to-do.

Then Lazy-lad sailed back again,
  And a wiser lad was he,
For he said, "I've wandered to every land
  That is in the geography;
And in each and all I've found that folks
  Are busy the whole year through,
And everybody in every place
  Seemed to have something to do.

"So it must be the best way, after all,
  And I mean to stay on shore,
And learn my lessons and do my tasks,
  And be Lazy-lad no more.
The busiest folks are the happiest,
  And what Mother said is true,
For I've found out there is no such place
  As the land of Nothing-to-do.

—Child's Hour.

TO THE BOYS

ONLY a few days ago while passing along the street I chanced to meet a little boy of eleven or twelve who ought to have been full of life and vigor, but instead seemed to have little ambition. You may

readily understand what caused this lack of interest in life when I. tell you that this dear boy was smoking a cigaret.

What blessings the boys are to this world! What should we do without them? for are they not the ones that make our noble men? How a mother's heart rejoices to look upon her son as he quickly grows from infancy to boyhood! He is the pride and joy of the home. With what tender care he is watched and protected and given all the educational privileges that can be afforded! What hopes spring to the father's heart when he realizes his boy is developing to manhood! He eagerly watches and fancies great possibilities in the future. A loving sister finds delight in his companionship. But ah! can you imagine the anguish of that mother's heart, the fond sister's sorrow, the father's blasted hopes, when they are informed that this boy is forming the cigaret habit? Can words express the sadness such intelligence brings to that home?

It is a common sight these days to see boys not over ten or eleven years old smoking. Little do they realize the harm they derive from

practising this filthy habit. They take into their systems such poisonous substances that every organ of their bodies is affected, and thus
they unfit themselves for properly performing the duties of life. And
yet many boys smoke because they think it makes them appear more
manly. What a wrong idea they have! Boys do not realize the danger
they are tampering with when they begin smoking, but feel assured
they can stop when they so desire; but, alas! they find this a task that
only few accomplish without help from God. How sad to see our rosy-
cheeked, merry-eyed, robust schoolboys exchanged for young men with
saddened features, faded cheeks, and diseased bodies yet this is the
exchange caused by the early use of tobacco.

I quote the substance of a magazine article containing truths that
should cause every boy and young man to think seriously before he
proceeds further in this degrading habit. "The cheap cigarets com-
monly smoked by boys contain a mixture of tobacco-quids, cigar-stumps,
opium, valerian, and other appetite-kindling drugs. The smoke of
this drugged mixture, combined with the smoke of the cigaret-paper,
is not only exhilarating but killing. In recent examinations in one of
the principal schools of Virginia, among the boys who smoked and
those who did not, it was found that the non-smoker averaged 86 and
those who smoked 75—eleven points lower."

Dear young friend, I would that these facts might awaken within
you, if you indulge in such a habit, a decision to stop while you may,
before it has enslaved you to the extent that you can not. If you have
not as yet begun, may you ever shun the temptation. The Lord has
promised to give grace sufficient to enable us to be overcomers. Let us
yield our young lives to him and commit ourselves to his keeping.

—*Frances B. Tallen.*

HABITS: WHAT THEY ARE

SOME one has said that a man's character is the sum of all his habits.
This being so, most people are a mixture of strength and weakness,
of good and bad—strong in some points and pitifully weak in others.
If the forming of good habits is the path to good character, the sooner
we realize what we are doing for ourselves day by day, the better it will
be for us. Because of the pleasure certain things afford them now,

some young people, not once thinking of the harm they are doing, go on forming habits that will shame and bind them in later years.

Habit is automatic action, and is made possible by doing an act over and over again. Things done through habit are done unconsciously or semi-consciously, and require little or no use of the will.

Here is a little boy just learning to dress himself. See what a task he has and what a puzzle to his childish brain to know how the different articles go on. But after a few weeks of practise the same boy will be able to dress himself automatically, talking all the time of something that has happened or is going to happen and that takes all his attention. The order of dressing has become a habit to him, so that he no longer has to use his will and attention to get his clothes on properly.

Here is a girl learning to play the piano. See her in her first lessons. How attentively she must watch the notes and her fingers in order to strike the proper keys! It takes a constant use of her will to compel her fingers to act properly and her eyes to read correctly. But after she has become proficient, she can play a piece of music correctly while her mind is far away on something else. Her fingers have formed the habit of acting as her eyes tell her how to act, and her eyes have formed the habit of reading the music without the use of the will.

Again, a lady has formed the habit of locking her door and hanging the key in a certain place whenever she leaves the house. This she does without any use of the will, but at first she had to keep constantly reminding herself of this or she would forget it.

All the habits we have spoken of are formed by doing the same thing over and over in the same way until the nerves and muscles act without calling on the will and with scarcely a thought to assist. This is the way all habits are formed, whether good or bad. Good habits usually require closer attention in the beginning, for bad habits are generally formed through carelessness.

Habits once formed are very hard to break, and one indulged in for years is almost impossible to break. So it is wisest to build good habits in the beginning, so that they will not have to be broken and made over.

From infancy we build life-habits; but especially from the age of ten or twelve to twenty, through these changing years when childhood is left behind and manhood and womanhood is entered, our life-habits are formed. Then, in this respect, these years are the most important years of our lives. "Life is too short to get over a bad habit."— *Sidney Smith*.

"Sow an act, and reap a habit;
Sow a habit, and reap a character;
Sow a character, and reap a destiny."
—*Boardman*.

—*Mabel Hale*.

HABITS: HOW TO FORM THE GOOD

A HABIT is formed by using the will to compel the performance of some act until the nerves and the muscles will carry the act on without calling for the will. Boys and girls can have command of their own wills. And because they can have command, it is possible for any of them to form good habits if they set themselves about it. The more the will is used, the stronger it becomes, and the more able to undertake great things. We all admire people with strong wills, and why should we not be what we admire, when it is possible by asserting our strength?

To form any habit we must do the act over and over. Doing an act just once or twice, or even half a dozen times, will not form a habit; the act must be done a great number of times. Take the habit of prompt obedience, than which there is no better recommendation for any one starting out in life. In order for one to possess this characteristic, one must practise prompt obedience hundreds of times. And to bring the will into use and compel one's self to obey promptly and regularly, takes force and decision. To do this makes one strong and noble. When called in the morning, get right up and dress quickly, not once in a while, but every time, till the thought of lingering is gone from the mind. If one will do this three hundred and sixty-five times a year for a few years, it will become a habit that can not be easily broken.

When sent on an errand, go at once without stopping to parley or argue. Do what is required and return as soon as possible. After a person has done this a hundred times or so, the habit becomes woven into his character, and people begin to call him a reliable person.

When forbidden to do a certain thing, even if you can not see why obey for the very sake of forming good character if for nothing else;

and when bidden by rightful authority to do certain things, try to do them to the very best of your understanding. You will then not only be pleasing the one who has bidden you, but also be forming another link in your strong chain of habits.

Another trait of character that we all admire is neatness and tidiness in the care of one's belongings. This characteristic is acquired by forming habits of neatness. It takes time and patience, but it is worth the trouble. Somebody must hang up John's best clothes, and why should not John hang them up when he takes them off? That would save his sister or mother the unpleasant job next morning, and besides, he would then know just where they were. It takes a bit of will-power to put everything away when one is tired or sleepy or chilly, but to do it is a long step towards becoming a tidy person.

Somebody must pick up the books and papers scattered about on tables and floors, must pick up the balls and marbles rolling about, must hang up the coats or caps, or hunt them when they are needed, must clean after the muddy boots—must keep things tidy about home, or we should all be ashamed. Why should not each one care for his own things? Putting things away when done with them, hanging up coat and cap, wiping the shoes at the door, keeping one's self combed and brushed and tidy, are all important little habits that go to form good character.

We all dislike a slack, careless workman. Yet there is not one such workman but might have been a good one if he had formed right habits as a boy. It takes real strength of character to stay in the potato-patch and pick up all when fishing is good, or to do the dishes just right when the girls are calling out to play, but that is the way the habit of thoroughness is formed. "If you would make a thing a habit, do it."—*Epicetus.*   —*Mabel Hale.*

HABITS: THE POWER OF THE BAD

"THE CHAINS of habit are, in general, too small to be felt till they are too strong to be broken."—*Samuel Johnson.*

"Man is chained to his deed like a prisoner to his ball."—*Tuscan Proverb.*

Were you to put your two wrists together and I to wrap a fine silk thread once around them you could snap it off and be free with scarcely an effort. But were I to wrap it around your wrists a number of times, you would find it difficult to break. If I should keep on wrapping, you could not break it at all, but would be helpless till some one set you free. This is equally true with a habit. You may do one little act of deceit, tell one small untruth, take one taste of tobacco, or drink one sup of liquor, and not be bound. But you commit the act again and again, till it has wound its cords about you so that it would take a real effort to free yourself. Yet you know you could if you would, and so you feel safe while the coils are being wrapped about you many more times. Then you try to throw them off, but you are tied fast. Such is the way of bad habits.

Were I to lightly fold a sheet of paper and then straighten it out again, I should find that it tended to fold again just where I folded it. Only with a hot iron could I smooth it out. If I folded it once more and pressed the crease, even though I might make it lie straight by using a hot iron, yet effects of the fold would remain. And each time I folded it, the less useful it would become, and the broader the crease would grow. So it is with habit. Do an act of wrong, and you find it easier to do the second time than it was the first. But it may be smoothed out by hard means until it is as if it had not happened. But keep repeating the act, and it will leave an indelible mark on the character. Eventually the scars will become so deep that even the forgiving grace of God can not remove them. Many men and women whose lives have been bruised and broken by bad habits, are serving God now the best they can, but the scars are left on both soul and body. Such persons can not be their best for God, for bad habits have ruined their best.

An Eastern fable tells of a young prince who raised a young lion, and, finding him weak and helpless, did not try to control him. Every day the little lion gained in strength and became harder to manage, until at last he became enraged and fell upon his master and killed him. So it is with many of the evil habits. At first they seem innocent and harmless, but after a while they grow to have the mastery, and they overcome the doers of them.

"He that soweth thistles shall reap prickles." "It is easier to prevent ill habits than to break them."—*Motto on Plato's ring.* "In the field of destiny we reap as we have sown."—*Whittier.* "Be not deceived; God is not mocked; for whatsoever a man soweth, that shall he also reap."—*Bible.* 					—*Mabel Hale.*

HABITS: THE BEAUTY OF WORK

A MAN'S character is formed by his habits. A man who has careless, idle habits is lacking in admirable character, and is often positively vicious. He is a slave to his habits, a make-believe man, a failure in nearly everything he undertakes. Even though he may inherit wealth he can not hold the respect of industrious men, but is looked upon as a fellow of little worth. On the other hand, a man who is careful and industrious, though he may never be rich in this world's goods, is known for his upright character and true worth. He is upheld by his good habits.

Every person who really amounts to anything in the world is a worker. He knows how to do some useful work well, and does it. Every boy and girl who would take a place among the noble and honored of earth must first learn to be useful at something. All good people must keep busy, and no idle person can keep good. To be of real value in the world's work, one must love work for its own sake, as well as for what it will bring. He must love to feel the responsibility of his part. To be such a worker, one must have habits of industry and carefulness.

It is good for every child, after the age of seven or eight, to have some work to do, something for which he is responsible. The work should not be hard enough to harm his little body, but it should be something that will help him begin to learn to have a part in the work of the great world. He will feel that he amounts to something if he has a part to perform. He should learn to do this work without being prompted. If the mother has to remind every one of the children of his or her work, and then see that it is done right, she would almost rather do it herself. In that case the child is of no real help, and besides, he is forming a careless habit that may stay with him for life. If John's part is to bring in the kindling and drive the cows, he should do those things without having to be told. If Mary's part is to wash the dishes and sweep the floor, she should do that without having to be prompted.

Many women are very unhappy because they have never learned to do anything that is of real use in the world. They can play a little on the piano, play hard at outdoor games, entertain their friends, dress up and look attractive, make a little fudge or cake, perhaps; but they do not know how to do one really useful thing. After a while they weary of being a butterfly, and can not be a bee. Life becomes very hard and dark for them, although they live in palaces and have much money.

How glad every little girl should feel who is taught how to work at something useful!

Every boy should learn some trade by which he can make a good living. He should learn to do something whereby he can be of service in the world's work. There is much that needs to be done, and there is a good, broad place for every one who will try. Every girl should learn, first of all, to be a good housewife, to cook and to sew, and to manage a house, and after that, if possible, to do some other useful work that might bring her employment if necessary. But, girls, be useful somewhere. Learn to work! Have a part in God's great plan! Who would be a drone, a nothing among the busy people of earth?

"In a general way, we get the places we are ready to fill." "Whatsoever is worth doing at all is worth doing well." "The only easy place is the grave."—*Beecher,* to a boy who wanted help to find an easy place.
                                                —*Mabel Hale.*

HABITS OF THOUGHT

"AS A MAN thinketh in his heart, so he is." A man is no better than the thoughts he habitually thinks. "Thoughts are things." It is hard to realize this, and as a consequence thoughts are often lightly considered. Evil thoughts are sometimes allowed to lodge in the mind unreproved till the whole man is polluted. Thoughts can be controlled. They can be made subject to one's will and to the will of God. Evil thoughts, neither light and chaffy ones, need be entertained.

Every thought makes, as it were, a tiny furrow in the brain. Each time a certain thought is repeated, that furrow is deepened, until it becomes easier for thought to follow that path than any other. If one continually dwells upon his troubles, he will see trouble in much that he looks at; but if one thinks of his blessings, he will be able to see blessings in that at which he looks. If one gives way to evil, bitter thoughts, it will become almost impossible for him to think any other kind. He will become as bitter as his thoughts. If one allows himself to think unclean and impure thoughts, he will soon come to see and hear only those things that tend to make him more impure in his thoughts.

If one entertains a good thought, it will make him able to think a stronger and a better thought, and again that better thought will make him able to think and act with more strength and courage·than he could possibly have done before. But if one gives way to an evil thought, a worse thought will be at its end, and a still worse one at the end of that one, till finally the evil thought will completely overcome him.

Thoughts show on the face like lines on a map. Sad thoughts make the face melancholy; bitter, envious thoughts make the face sour and peevish; low, unclean thoughts make the face ashamed and unable to look pure people in the face; pure, happy thoughts make the face bright and attractive.

To have good thought-habits, one must continually fill the mind with good things. This can be done by pure conversation, good reading, useful work and study. Every one is tempted to evil thoughts by those things that must be met in the world. Evil literature, impure companions, gossip, slander—all these are about us and must be avoided; the thoughts they arouse must be thrown off. If evil thoughts persist in coming into your consciousness, turn to something worth while to think about. If they come at night, by will-power think of other· things. If you can not overcome them that way, get up and walk about. Fight hard, and you will win the battle. Ask God to help you keep pure. Form good thought-habits while you are children and young people, and evil thoughts will not bother you when you are old.

—Mabel Hale.

OUR HABITS: BRAVERY IN LITTLE THINGS

WITH what pleasure we hear the account of an act of bravery and how honored we feel if it is one of our own relatives who has been so courageous! Better still if we ourselves have performed some really brave act. Some boys and girls have great day-dreams of the brave things they might do, and really long for something terrible to happen so that they may have a chance to prove their courage. If only they might be present when there is a fire, or when some one is drowning, or when a horse is running away, and be the one to rush in and rescue those in danger!

But the opportunities to do great deeds of valor come so seldom that to one expecting to be really courageous in great deeds only, life may seem very dull and scarcely worth the living. When I hear great longing for large opportunities expressed, I think of an adage I once read: "It takes more than one white stocking to robe a man in pure white robes." So it takes more than one act of courage to make a person really brave. The truest courage, the bravest hearts, the noblest deeds, are often right before our eyes, and we fail to see them because we think the person is only doing his duty. But really, it takes more actual courage to do one's duty always than it does to spring forward and stop a running horse, or even to go into a burning building and rescue one from the flames. Such deeds of courage win the applause of the people and have a charm and excitement which is wholly lacking in plain duty.

Pride, excitement, and ambition may push one on to do great deeds, but it requires genuine pluck to stay by sober duty. To say no to temptation even when the tempter is our best friend; to be obedient when no one would know of our disobedience; to speak gently even when one is vexed and tired; to go on giving up one's cherished hopes for the pleasure of some one else; to speak kindly and graciously to an old person in the street when your comrades are going on ahead and are laughing at you besides; to be kind and thoughtful to little children; to be a true lady or gentleman in the face of ridicule and personal inconvenience—these show more real courage than does the performing of some thrilling act. Moreover, when one trains his body and mind to obey his sense of right and duty, he is preparing himself in the best way possible to do the one brave deed when the chance appears.

—*Mabel Hale.*

THE HABIT OF ATTENTION

ATTENTION is the power or faculty that enables one to concentrate one's thoughts on the thing in hand. By it all our energies may be centered on one thing. Constant use of this faculty will result in the formation of a habit. Though this is a habit hard to acquire, yet it is one that will liberally repay every effort spent in forming it.

The reason why boys and girls forget so many things that they are expected to do is because they fail to give proper attention. Just mention to Mary that she may wear a new dress at a certain time, and she will not forget to do so, for she paid attention to what was said; tell her to put on her apron when she comes from school, and she will more than likely forget, since she paid little heed. In the first place, she wants to wear the new dress, and that interests her; but the wearing of an apron is a bother, and she leaves the responsibility on her mother. This sort of forgetting is not really honest.

Babies and small children can pay attention only to what interests them; but as a child grows older he can begin to have power over his faculty of attention. When he is ten or twelve years old he can, by the use of his will, make himself pay good heed to very uninteresting things. It is this attention coupled with the will that really develops boys and girls into men and women of strong character. If one should remain like a child, paying heed only when something amused or interested him, he could never rise to any real worth in the world.

School-children can develop the power of attention by voluntarily paying heed to all that is said in class. One who reads can develop this good habit by reading that which makes him think, and thinking while he reads. After reading a paragraph or two, stop and think it over, and if you can not recall it, read it again. Make the mind pay heed to what it is doing.

Children in the home can develop this habit by listening to what is told them and trying to carry out the commands and requests exactly as they were made.

Many a mishap and bitter moment would be avoided if one always paid attention. The habit of attention is worth more to a boy than a pocketful of money or the favors of many family friends. If, when he seeks work, people see that he pays heed to what he is doing and really tries he will need but little further recommendation. A boy with half the ability but with the habit of attention can accomplish more by far than his gifted brother who is careless and heedless. —*Mabel Hale.*

READING-HABITS AND THEIR EFFECTS

THE WORLD is full of reading-matter. There is no need of any one's going through life uninstructed, for profitable and instructive reading is in reach of every one. But with the good reading is a great amount of that which is bad. This bad reading is to the mind just what poison is to the body.

Our taste for reading is, to a very great extent, governed by what we allow ourselves to read. There is nothing else in which we can so quickly form habits as in our taste for reading, nor is there anything

much harder to break than a bad reading-habit. If we read fiction of
an exciting and adventurous nature, in which the heroes and heroines
are found in unthought-of and dangerous predicaments, and exciting
escapes and escapades occur, it makes our even and uneventful lives
seem very dull. Such stories tend to excite the young and cause them
to live in an unreal world, in which they try to produce some of the
conditions described in their beloved stories. Such persons are discontented with things as they are, and long for excitement. This is the
reason why many boys run away, and why many crimes are committed
by the young. And if a boy allows himself to form a taste for this
kind of reading, all other will seem dry and dull. Though he might be
able to read at one sitting a whole book of such fiction, yet a dozen
pages of history or biography would tire him. He can not keep his
mind on it, because he has formed a habit that makes it almost impossible for him to think seriously as he reads. He wants to feel more
than think.

If a girl allows herself to form the habit of reading love-stories,
she will develop an appetite for them that will be almost as hard to control as the appetite for strong drink, and nearly as injurious to mind
and body. The love-stories and novels that deal almost entirely with
romance put thoughts and feelings into the mind and heart of a girl,
that should have no place there. She develops too quickly in the ro-
mantic, affectionate part of her nature, and, like all things that grow
too rapidly, she becomes weakened by her premature growth. We see
silly, simpering, giggling, love-sick girls looking and longing for some
great experience such as their heroines in the stories have had, and
weaving about themselves a foolish cloud of dreams that makes the
every-day world seem a very poor place to live in. This giddy condition of mind makes a girl unable to appreciate things that are good and
pure, and puts a false beauty on things that are really impure. Girls,
if you would be good, pure, sensible girls, leave alone all reading that
excites your nature and makes you discontented with homes and loved
ones. Such reading is ruinous to both peace of mind and good morals.

The reading of pure, instructive literature forms a habit for itself,
and also feeds and builds up the mind and strengthens the morals. If
we remember that our books are our friends and that a person will
become like the company he keeps, then we can see the danger of impure reading.   —*Mabel Hale.*

A GIANT ALL SHOULD FIGHT

BOYS and girls like to hear and read stories about giants. There is hardly a person in this country who has not heard of Jack the Giant-killer. Though his wonderful history is not true, still it is very interesting.

David, a giant-killer, was a real person. He actually lived about

three thousand years ago. Goliath, the giant he killed, was a real, live giant. He was nearly ten feet high. We have read about several of the giant's brothers that were killed in David's time. The whole family of them, you will remember, w a s destroyed.

But the giants are not all dead yet. There are giants on the earth in these days. They are not men with huge bodies, f o u r or five times larger than common-sized men; t h e y are great sins, and God expects us all to try to fight them.

The first giant I wish to speak of is Giant Selfishness. He is a very ugly-looking creature. If he could be caught in bodily shape and be carried to some place where his picture might be taken, I am sure that when you came to look at it, you would think him about the ugliest creature you have ever seen.

God has given each of us two eyes, two ears, two hands, and two feet. He thus reminds us that we are to see and hear and work and walk for others as well as for ourselves. But he has given you but one mouth; for you are to eat for yourself only, and not for others.

But Giant Selfishness never sees nor hears nor does anything for any one but himself. If we had a correct likeness of him, we should see a great one-eyed, one-eared, one-armed monster, with his other eye and ear and arm shriveled and dried up for want of use.

The business of this giant is to take people prisoners. He likes especially to do this while they are young, making a brother unkind even to his sisters. He binds his chains on them, and then drags them to his castle. If they stay there long, they will begin to grow just like him—ugly, one-sided looking creatures. I do not mean to say that this change takes place in their bodies, but it does in their souls. They learn to love none but themselves. They think and care for none but themselves.

But if this giant does not appear in bodily form, how may we know when he is trying to fasten his chains on us, and make us his prisoners? Let me tell you.

If you find you are learning to think more of yourself than of others, then be sure the giant is after you. If you see boys or girls enter a room and go and take the best seat in it when older persons are present; if you see them pick out for themselves the largest piece of cake or the biggest and finest apples when these are handed around, you may be sure Giant Selfishness is at work on them. If they do not take care, he will soon make them his prisoners.

Now, we must all fight this giant. But how are we to do this? We must make it a close hand-to-hand fight. We must seize him and wrestle with him. We must fight this giant by self-denial.   —*Selected.*

STICK TO IT

HOW MANY times the bird that is building its nest flies to and fro with twigs and bits of straw! Day by day it perseveres until the nest is finished.

So, too, the spider spins up and down, this way and that, making her web. If some one sweeps it away when it is finished, she patiently spins again until the web is once more complete.

If the bird or the spider ceased working when obstacles presented themselves, there would be no nests for young birds and no spider-webs.

Boys and girls, what a lesson can be learned from these little workers! What they do from instinct you can do from principle. Do you find it hard to be neat, or truthful, or obedient? Do not give up, but when you fail begin again. No good thing is done without effort.

—*Exchange.*

WHOSE PLACE WILL YOU TAKE?

When mechanic, physician, and teacher have passed;
When the lips of the statesman are silent at last;
When the drunkard has reeled from the bar to the grave,
And we miss from their seats the gay scoundrel and knave—
Tell me, then, as the ranks of life widen and break,
Whose place will you take, lad? Whose place will you take?

Here's the farmer's boot soiled by the acres he tilled;
Here's a glove that the hand of a gambler once filled;
Here's the miller's grain-cap, the chief justice's gown,
And the coat of a citizen loved by the town;
Here's the lazy man's chair and the loafer's old shoes;
They have left them for you, lad; pray, which do you choose?

Up the mountain of life are new steeps to explore;
On the streets of life many an unopened door;
There's a song of life yet with new notes to be sung;
There's a future that waits for the hearts of the young:
Then what are you fitting for? Whose place to take?
And what place will you make, lad? What place will you make?

—*Selected.*

RAISE YOUR OWN BEES

IF YOU should stand near a beehive, you would see a very busy family at work. Have you ever thought of comparing your home to a hive and yourself to a bee? If the bees are noted for their industry, there are many reasons why children should be so in a far greater degree.

In every hive there is a queen who rules, and in your hive you could be the queen who should "improve each shining hour."

Now, if you are the queen what shall the bees be who are to work with you? Suppose we place them in your hive in the order of their importance:

Bee Obedient is a very busy little worker and a very necessary helper to the queen. When your mother says, "Do this" or "Don't do that," Bee Obedient will be right there to help you.

Bee Kind is perhaps the next important one. This busy little Bee usually works overtime in every home-hive, without having any special duty assigned.

There is a stir in your hive as Bee Useful enters, and he keeps things humming for the Queen.

The next bee is not content to work only in the hive; as for that matter, they all usually follow the queen wherever she goes. It is Bee Industrious, who watches golden opportunities, no matter whether in school or in the hive or out in the big garden called the world.

Bee Loving settles in the very heart of the hive and stirs all the others up until the hive is filled with a glow. But still there is room for ever so many more, and these new ones will surely follow the others into the hive. There are Bee Sincere, Bee Honest, Bee Tactful, Bee Quick.   —*Selected*.

HOW TO CONQUER GIANT SELFISHNESS

THERE were two little boys named James and William. One day as they were just starting for school their father gave them each a five-cent piece to spend as they liked. The little fellows were very much pleased with this, and went off as merry as crickets.

"What are you going to buy, William?" said James after they had walked a little way.

"I don't know," William replied; "I have not thought yet. What are you going to buy?"

"Why, I tell you what I believe I'll do. You know mother is sick. Now, I believe I'll buy her a nice orange. I think it will taste good to her."

"You may do so if you please, James," said William; "but I'm going to buy something for myself. Father gave me the money to spend for myself, and I mean to do it. If mother wants an orange, she can send for it. She has money, and Hannah gets everything she wants.''

"I know that," said James, "but then it would make me feel so happy to see her eating an orange that I had bought for her with my own money. She is always doing something for us, or getting us some nice thing, and I want to let her see that I don't forget it.''

"Do as you please," said William, "but I go in for the candy." Presently they came to a confectioner's shop.

William spent his five cents for cream candy; but James bought an orange. When they went home at noon, he went into his mother's chamber and said: "See, Mama, what a nice orange I have brought for you!''

"It is indeed very nice, my son, and it will taste very good to me. I have been wanting an orange all the morning. Where did you get it?''

"Father gave me five cents this morning, and I bought it with that.''

"You are very good, my dear boy, to think of your sick mother. And you wouldn't spend your money for cakes or candy, but denied yourself, that you might get an orange for me. Mother loves you for this exercise of self-denial.'' And she threw her arms around his neck and kissed him.

Now, you see how Giant Selfishness made an attack on these two boys. James fought him off bravely by the exercise of self-denial. William refused to exercise self-denial, and so the giant got a hitch of his chain around him. We shall find this giant making attacks upon us all the time. We can fight him off only by self-denial.   —*Selected.*

FOR MOTHER

HE WAS only a mite of a boy, dirty and ragged, and he had stopped for a little while in one of the city's free play-grounds to watch a game of ball between boys of his own and a rival neighborhood. Tatters and grime were painfully in evidence on every side, but this little fellow attracted the attention of a group of visitors, and one of them, reaching over the child's shoulder as he sat on the ground, gave him a luscious golden pear. The boy's eyes sparkled, but the eyes were his only thanks as he looked back to see from whom the gift had come, and then turned his face away again, too shy or too much astonished to speak.

But from that time on his attention was divided between the game and his new treasure. He patted the pear, he looked at it, and at last, as if to assure himself that it was as delicious as it appeared, he lifted it to his lips and cautiously bit out a tiny piece near the stem. Then, with a long sigh of satisfaction and assurance, he tucked the prize safely inside his dirty little blouse.

"Why don't ye eat it, Tony?" demanded a watchful acquaintance.

"Eat it? All meself? Ain't I savin' it for me mother?"

The tone, with its mingling of resentment and loyalty, made further speech unnecessary. Whatever else Tony lacked, and it seemed to be nearly everything, he had learned humanity's loftiest lesson; he held another dearer than self, and knew the joy of sacrifice.—*Selected.*

"WHERE THE FIGHT IS HOTTEST"

[The following, from a boy in a training-camp, shows that the writer well understands how to win in the greatest of conflicts.—Ed.]

IT IS in a boy's own soul that *the fight is hottest*. "He that ruleth his spirit is better than he that taketh a city." Every boy has his temptations, and in the silence of his own heart go on the struggles which shall decide whether he is to be a winner or a loser in life.

Many a boy wishes he did not have temptations. He thinks he could be the fellow he ought to be if some allurement were not always drawing him aside from the path of right. But let him remember that no temptation has ever made him go astray. Temptation makes a boy neither weak nor strong, but it shows how good a fighter he is. It is only a moral coward who says, "If God wants me to be right and decent and fit for anything, why does he permit me to be tempted?"

"It takes more character and manhood," some one has said, "to be fit for one's country than to fight for her." Who are the really fit and noble Americans? They are

> "Men who never fail their brothers,
> Men who never shame their mothers,
> Men who stand for country, home, and God."

The boy who wins the battle where *the fight is hottest* will become such a man. But to win this fight in the soul, a boy needs more than his own strength. The great men who have been trying to help boys in

this fight with themselves have learned that it is only by letting Jesus come into their lives and make them strong that they are able to become conquerors over temptation.

It is no dishonor or sin for a boy to be tempted. It is merely a case of God trusting him, testing him, to see whether the boy will live up to what he trusts him to be. Think of it! God trusts you when you are tempted. He hopes you will stand the test so that he can trust you more— give you more to do for him.

Temptation measures what you are. It tests your trueness, worthwhileness, your virtue, cleanness, ambitions, and all else there is of you. To stand true to Jesus when tempted will make a boy stronger, but to yield to the temptation will make him weaker. Do you want God to be pleased with you and trust you? Then stand true to him when you are tempted. —*Donald Achor.*

THE DEADLY CIGARET

SEVERAL years ago, in a quiet, rural district in the lower part of
the State of Michigan, John P— lived a peaceful life in his early
school-days. His life should have been a happy one, as his parents,
though not wealthy, did all they could to make home attractive. His
parents were praying people; they had found Christ as their Savior,
and tried to train their boy, both by precept and example, in the way
of righteousness. But, like many other boys, he fell under the evil
influences of wicked and vicious companions, and from them learned
evil things that dragged him down in the course of sin. In spite of his
father's and mother's instructions and entreaty, he grew more sinful,
and more tired of the home life, until one bleak day in January he "ran
away" and went out into the cold, wicked world to make his own way.
Satan was on the alert to drag him down, and his evil associates helped
to accomplish Satan's design.

One of the evil habits that this boy had learned at school soon
fastened itself upon him—he had learned the use of tobacco in various
forms—and instead of finding the pleasure that he had thought he
would, he awoke to the fact that he was a slave. When he sought deliverance
from cigaret-smoking—one of the most deadly of the habits
that are destroying many young lives today—he found that he had not
only the tobacco-habit to deal with, but also the tendencies which lead
to the use of strong drink.

So life dragged on for a number of years. But his mother, who
firmly believed in the power of prayer, still continued to hold on to
God for her boy. God was taking notice of her prayers, and at last in
a distant city in another State her son turned to God, who delivered
him from all his evil habits and saved him from all his sins. Sin, however,
had left its influences on his life; and today he has many severe
battles with the enemy of his soul that he would not experience had
he not formed those evil habits. As he reflects on the past and thinks
of the terrible effects that cigarets had on his early life, he often longs
to sound the warning to the young to shun these deadly things as they
would shun a door to the pit of hell itself.

Tobacco companies and cigaret manufacturers are very diligent
in their efforts to advertise their goods, and are spending millions of
dollars to get their wares before the public. We sometimes see children
playing with the papers that are used for rolling cigarets. Parents

do not seem to think that there is any harm in their doing so. "They are only papers," they say. But the handling of these papers is an incentive to the making of the real article.

Cigarets are often called "coffin-nails," and they may well be so called. I have been told that in a certain asylum there are 153 boys who are insane, and that *every one of them was a cigaret-smoker*. In the Chicago Parental School there are about 360 boys. They were sent there because of their waywardness and of their parents' inability to control them. Of the 360 boys, there are but 35 who are not cigaret-smokers, or 325 who do smoke.

As I write these lines, I have before me some literature from the Anti-Cigarette League of America. It tells some dreadful tales of the ravages of the accursed cigarets on the youth of our land. The cigaret has been the most powerful agent in effecting the great increase in the number of offenses against the law by boys in the last five years. This is the opinion of Judge Stubbs, who was for a long time the Judge of the Juvenile Court of Indianapolis. He also says: "I have had before me more than six hundred boys who were smokers of cigarets, most of whom have become cigaret-fiends. I have found, also, that in nearly every case where the offense was of a grievous, criminal, or degrading nature, the defendant was a user of cigarets. . . . When a boy becomes addicted to the use of cigarets, the disease is in his blood and brain; his moral fiber is gone; he becomes apathetic, listless, and indifferent; his vitality is sapped away and all the vigor that should characterize the normal boy is gone."

Here is something from the pen of a doctor in Michigan: "A schoolboy only twelve years of age died from excessive cigaret-smoking. During his delirium he continually asked for cigarets and matches, going through the motions of lighting a cigaret." This physician also tells of a boy ten years of age whose father was a cigaret-smoker. The father taught the boy to smoke when five years old. Because of this, the child was so stunted in body that he was no larger than a boy six years old, and he had never been able to learn his letters so that he could remember them from one day to the next.

Not only do cigarets themselves cause much havoc, but they are almost certain to lead to the drink-habit. Very few who are accustomed to cigaret-smoking do not crave strong drink. And through the combined influences of smoking and drinking there is left behind a wake of suffering and misery that affects not only the victim but also his family and friends.

If you who are reading these lines are already in the grip of this terrible fiend, I am glad to tell you that there is a way to be freed. You will find the cure in Christ, who can set the captive at liberty, can break every chain that binds. It may take a struggle on your part, but through prayer and help from God you will find deliverance. Boys and girls, forever decide that by God's grace you will have absolutely nothing to do with these deadly things. Heed this advice of the apostle Paul: "Let no man despise thy youth; but be thou an example in purity."   —*V. A. Wilcox.*

TWO KINDS OF BOYS

BOYS may be tall or short; they may have blue eyes or brown eyes or eyes of some other color; they may have black or light, straight or curly hair; they may wear good clothes or very poor clothes; and they may differ in many other ways; but, after all, such things do not matter much. There are really only two kinds of boys in the world —the boys who are polite and the boys who are not polite.

The polite boy is kind to his brothers and sisters; he is respectful to older persons; if he has a little sister, he is quick to protect her in time of danger and always thoughtful of her comfort; if he has pets, he is good to them, and to all animals, including cats and dogs. The polite boy doesn't become angry when something happens to displease him; he is cheerful and willing to lend a hand when help is needed, but he is not always pushing himself to the front and making his presence obnoxious. He enjoys his outdoor sports, and can run and shout with the best of the boys; but he does not make a playground of the side-walk, and expect grown-up persons to step aside in order that he may enjoy a monopoly of conveniences intended for the general public. The polite boy, in short, remembers that there are other people in the world beside himself, and that they have rights which he should respect; and because he keeps this in mind, he is everywhere held in high esteem, and his presence is desired.

The impolite boy is the reverse of all this; not usually because he is unkind at heart, but simply because he doesn't think. He has much of the "don't care" spirit about him. He enjoys teasing his sisters,

and never stops to think how they feel about it; and there is so much
fun for him in coasting down a long sidewalk that it never occurs to him
that elderly and perhaps feeble persons using the walk for its legiti-
mate purpose, can not easily avoid being run over. The impolite boy
wears the kind of cap that doesn't come off, and if he is greeted on the
street, the only answer he knows how to give is a careless nod with his
eyes turned away. He is noisy and boisterous about the house, and acts
as if he were the only occupant of it whose needs were of any consequence. So also in other matters. The impolite boy has his mind centered on himself, and is largely oblivious of the comfort and happiness
of others.

Which of the two classes of boys would be the pleasanter to have
around? The answer is not difficult. But why can not all boys be
polite? They have only to try in order to succeed, at least in a measure.
Perhaps they would try if they once gave the matter a serious thought.
Sometimes boys of really kind hearts are thoughtless and impolite
without meaning to be. They fail to see the importance of those little
attentions to the comforts of others that go so far toward making life
pleasant. They are likely to think it unmanly to trouble with such
things. They like to play the part of men; but they forget that the
outstanding marks of the fully developed man are gentleness, thoughtfulness, and true heart-courtesy toward all, but especially toward the
weak. Strength has its fulfilment in gentleness. The two belong
together.

> *"The bravest are the tenderest,*
> *The loving are the daring."*

It was the brave Sir Philip Sidney, the hero of many a battle-field, who,
lying sorely wounded and burning with thirst, nevertheless passed the
proffered cup of cold water to a soldier lying by his side; it was Sir
Walter Raleigh, admiral, discoverer, and literator, who threw his cloak
over a muddy crossing in order that a lady might pass over without
wetting her feet; and it was a greater than these, even the Lord Jesus
himself, who could hold multitudes spellbound by his marvelous elo-
quence, who could cure all manner of diseases, and even bring the dead
to life—it was he who looked lovingly on the mothers with little babes
in their arms, and said, "Suffer the little children to come unto me, and
forbid them not: for of such is the kingdom of God."

Then, boys, try to be kind and gentle. It will not make prigs or milksops of you; but it will make you strong, manly boys that every one will love.   —*M. E. Olsen.*

A BOY'S EXPERIENCE IN CIGARET-SMOKING

WHEN I was a small boy going to school, I one day saw an older boy smoking. This I thought looked manly. I began to inquire into the matter, and some bad boys told me that it really did look manly and that if I would smoke it would make a man of me. As I wanted to be a man as soon as possible, I decided to try that way.

First I attempted to smoke a pipe, but soon found that it was too strong for me. Then I began to look for something milder. At last I learned that the cigaret was mild; so I began to smoke one now and then whenever I could get with boys who used them. Erelong I began to buy tobacco and cigaret-papers, and to smoke frequently, not realizing the danger I was in. I would hear older people talk about habits forming and fastening their awful clutches on a person, but I thought I could quit at any time and so only laughed at their seemingly foolish remarks. But sad to say, erelong I woke up to the sad truth of the matter.

Later I learned that cigaret-papers contain various poisons. I also learned that when cigaret-smoke is inhaled it leaves more or less of these poisons, as well as poison from the tobacco itself, in the lungs. I well remember my first few attempts to inhale the smoke. It seemed to me as if coals of fire were burning my very lungs out. I gasped for breath. This was on account of the effect the poisons had on the lungs. Soon, by steady practise, I was able to inhale without much pain, and before long the appetite so fastened itself upon me that I inhaled the smoke because I was compelled to do so, although at first I inhaled it only because I thought the act "looked great."

When smoke is inhaled it leaves the poisonous nicotine on the lungs. This is shown by the difference in the appearance of smoke not inhaled and that which has been; smoke that has been inhaled has a clearer, whiter cast than that which has not been. Also, it can be proved in this way: When smoke not inhaled is blown hard with a little moisture from the breath on a white cloth, a brownish-yellow spot will remain. This is nicotine. But not so with smoke that has been inhaled, because the lungs have already absorbed the nicotine. Once I put a small speck of this nicotine in a cat's eye. Soon I could notice that a skum had formed over the eye.

I learned that after smoking one brand of tobacco I cared nothing for any other brand. It did not have the right taste, and I really detested any other than that to which I was accustomed. This also had a tendency to bind the cigaret habit. I soon was distinguished by my friends as a cigaret-fiend. This they could tell by the nicotine on the tips of my fingers. My finger-tips became a brownish color. This was caused by my holding the cigaret while smoking. The paper would become wet, and as the smoke came through and came in contact with the moist paper some of the nicotine would stay on the paper and go through on the fingers. This stain can not be washed off; it stays like a brand.

I soon became drowsy, seemingly having no energy. I had a tired, wearisome expression in my eyes. Now I could begin to see that cigarets were sapping out my very life. I realized when attempting to sing that my voice was failing. There seemed to be a tickling in my throat, and my lungs would give way so I would be compelled to stop. I also soon awoke to the fact that I was becoming very nervous. Things that in the past never had the least tendency to excite me now seemed to unstring every nerve. I could not sleep well at night. Some nights it seemed as though sleep would leave entirely. Then I discovered that by smoking just before retiring, also after retiring, I could quiet my nerves for a time and sleep sounder and rest better.

I would sometimes awaken in the still hours of the night and find it utterly impossible to go to sleep without smoking. No matter how cold the night, I was compelled to arise and smoke, or remain awake the rest of the night. A smoke was also the first thing in the morning. Nothing would go right until that appetite was satisfied. The same thing occurred after each meal. I was now fully awakened to the fact that I was a slave to the awful cigaret-habit. My health was fast failing. The dreaded disease catarrh had now overtaken me, and I was suffering very much from it. I knew it was caused from smoking. In despair I opened my eyes, only to view the fact that my friends were pointing the finger of scorn at me; those of high society who had been my former friends were now shunning me, caring no longer for my company. And I learned that cigaret-smokers can not obtain a reliable position on account of this habit. All the future truly looked black as night.

From Bad to Worse

When I found myself shut out from good society, I began to pursue some other course for enjoyment. The enemy, taking advantage of me, suggested that a few good novels would be a great benefit to one who at times felt so blue. Not knowing that they also are very injurious to the mind, I decided to try them. Soon I found that cigarets, novels, and I were going hand in hand to hell; that these two habits— cigaret-smoking and novel-reading—were two of the most binding habits I could form. They, if followed long enough, will so completely ruin the mind that the victim will care to do nothing else. I found it was very difficult to collect my thoughts. I became forgetful, and there seemed to be a carelessness over me that I could not overcome. I tried to get my mind once more settled on the affairs of life, but all in vain. Only a miserable failure followed every attempt. Then I would smoke harder and to such excess that my lungs would become so sore I would experience intense pain in the attempt to inhale the smoke. But I was bound and this poison must go to those lungs or I was "dead on my feet."

Here I began to awaken to the fact that I was reaping what I had sown. I began to think over my deplorable condition, and it was deplorable indeed. The devil, again taking the advantage of me, pointed out all my bad qualities, and showed me what a miserable creature I was, saying that my health was ruined, my character gone, my name disgraced, etc. He reminded me of how cruelly I had treated my dear parents and in conclusion said that of course I was so bound that I could never reform or amount to anything again, and that the best thing I could do was to get out of this world as soon as possible—to end my life by my own hand. I decided to commit suicide, thinking there were but few who would care. But ah! it was then I realized my unpreparedness. Thoughts of the hereafter came rolling up before my vision, and I shrank from it in terror. Sad indeed was my condition—I did not want to live and was afraid to die. God only knows what I suffered in this dreadful state of mind.

I was now fully decided that I did not want to die in that condition, but I realized that the awful monster death was on my track and

would soon overtake me if something was not done at once. It seemed
he was already staring me in the face like a hungry wolf. A total
wreck both soul and body, I realized I must, if possible, make a change.
I attempted to quit, resolving with a solemn oath never again to repeat
the act of smoking; but within a few hours or perhaps a day or so I
experienced failure. Then I would repeat the attempt, turn over a new
leaf, but erelong it was marred and black as night with another miserable failure. I now realized I had lost my will-power—the thing which
I would not, that I did, and that which I would, I did not.

Many are the times when I would repeat these words to myself,
"The wages of sin is death and bitter remorse, and surely I have found
it so." My health was gone; I was unable to do a hard day's work;
and I was bound to the cigaret habit by chains that God alone could
break. I fully realized that without the help of a higher power than
I possessed, I was, at the age of eighteen, a ruined boy.

Deliverance through Christ

It was in this sad hour that Jesus, in his mercy, proved his love
for me. I was almost ashamed to call upon him for help, having for
so long trampled his mercies under my feet. I thought of my dear
father and mother. Although far away, I knew that every day a prayer
was offered in my behalf. This thought was the first ray of hope that
made its appearance across my path of gloom. Oh, thank God for
praying parents! At this thought my soul cried to God for mercy.
The answer came, "Come unto me, all ye that labor and are heavy-
laden, and I will give you rest." I promised the Lord that if he would
only save my soul, my days, whether few or many, should be spent in
his service and his alone. Praise his name! then and there that great
mountain of sin rolled away. My soul was as free as heaven. I hardly
knew myself, I felt so happy.

But the burden of sin was not all he took away. He also removed
the very appetite and every desire for cigarets. I can never praise him
enough for what he did for me. And I can say in the fear of God, I
have never from that day had one temptation to smoke a cigaret.

The Lord also healed me of catarrh, which I had contracted
through smoking, and gave me back my voice; in fact, every part of
my body is stronger than it ever was in my life before. In a short time
I regained the confidence of my friends. Those who once looked upon

me as fallen, as a "warning against cigarets," were now making remarks about the wonderful change that had taken place in my life, and would encourage me by telling me it was the best thing I had ever done.

By constant prayer and careful living erelong I had once more the confidence of nearly all. But had it not been for a merciful Savior and had I not acted on my better judgment just when I did, no doubt I should tonight have been numbered not only with the dead but, ah!—with the LOST.

Dear reader, if you should be in the condition I was in, let me warn you: you are on very slippery ground. In Jesus' name I exhort you to turn *now*.   —*Clarence E. Bright.*

HAVE COURAGE, MY BOY, TO SAY NO

You're starting, my boy, on life's journey
  Along the grand highway of life;
You'll meet with a thousand temptations;
  Each city with evil is rife.
This world is a stage of excitement;
  There's danger wherever you go,
But if you are tempted in weakness,
  Have courage, my boy, to say no.

In courage alone lies your safety.
  When you the long journey begin,
Your trust in a heavenly Father
  Will keep you unspotted from sin.
Temptations will go on increasing
  As streams from a rivulet flow,
But if you'd be true to your manhood
  'Have courage, my boy, to say no.

Be careful in choosing companions;
  Seek only the brave and the true,
And stand by your friends when in trials,
  Never changing the old for the new;
And when by false friends you are tempted
  The taste of the wine-cup to know,
With firmness, with patience and kindness
  Have courage, my boy, to say no.

                                        —*Selected.*

BE KIND TO THE AGED

TO BE kind and respectful to elderly people is to win the favor of God and bring upon one's head benedictions and rich blessings. The Lord said, ''Thou shalt rise up before the hoary head, and honor the face of the old man, and fear thy God: I am the Lord.''

Children, God marks well your attitude and behavior toward those of older years. When they come into the room or car where you are sitting so comfortably he notices if you willingly and cheerfully rise and offer your seat. Never jostle them rudely in passing by, but if accidentally you should do so, then take special care to apologize. Be quick to pick up the fallen cane, to get the old man's hat, to hunt the lost article, to bring the cup of cold water, to carry the heavy load, to steady the trembling arm, and to speak comfortingly and respectfully always. Few people will be surer to appreciate these kind attentions and respectful manners than the aged. Here is an incident that will illustrate it.

An elderly man, who I think was a colored man, was one day passing along a street with a heavy load upon his shoulder. He dropped something, which fell into the gutter. Some young men who were standing near offered no assistance, but only laughed at his distress. A well-dressed lady passing by saw the situation, quietly stepped into the street, and with her gloved hand picked up the article and handed it to the aged man. As he was trying to thank her, his hat fell off and rolled into the street. She again stepped into the street, picked up his hat, and handed that to him. ''God bless you!'' he said from the depths of an appreciative heart. By this simple act of kindness the old man was made happier, the lady was surely happier, and these young men, we hope, received a lesson that will make their lives happier if they profit by it.

No matter what faults elderly people may have nor how near manhood or womanhood you may be, always speak to them intreatingly rather than reproachfully or in a faultfinding way. God's Word says, ''Rebuke not an elder, but intreat him as a father; and the elder women as mothers.'' Be patient and forbearing with their mistakes and weaknesses. We too may be old some day, and shall we not be glad then to have somebody be kind and patient with us?

God's unchangeable law is that what we sow we shall also reap. If we are kind and thoughtful of others, others will be of us; if we are

rude, thoughtless, and inconsiderate of others it will surely come back to us—if not now, sometime it will. So let us follow after and cultivate goodness, righteousness, trueness, love, kindness, and courtesy, and so enthrone these noble qualities of character within our hearts that the opposite kind—thoughtlessness, selfishness, unkindness, greed, and unfaithfulness—will find no place there.

I have known and heard of many children who became so untrue to filial affection that when their parents were old they begrudged them a home and care. Some have even covetously obtained possession of their parents' property and then neglected or refused to care for them.

An aged, palsied father lived with his son. Because of the trembling hands the poor old man often broke his dishes while eating, so he was provided with a wooden bowl in which to eat his victuals. One day the little grandson was whittling something with his knife. His father asked, "What are you making, my son?"

"A bowl for you to eat in, Papa, when you are old like Grandpa."

"This law is true, that the deeds you do
Shall ever come back to you;
Then sow, as you go, in life's fertile row
The kind that will profit you."

—*Anna M. Greeley.*

ARE YOU A SLAVE?

HAVE you ever heard of a galley-slave? Galleys were boats used by European nations many years ago. They were often large seagoing vessels, but were propelled partly or wholly by oars. The rowing was done by slaves or criminals. These men were called galley-slaves. Their lives were very sad. So hard and so constant was their work that they lived only a few years. They were chained to their oars, and it was impossible for them to free themselves.

There have been slaves in many nations, and our hearts throb with sympathy when we read of their bondage. Some may draw a breath of relief and say: "Thank God, the day of slavery is past. Today all men on American soil are free." Do not be deceived. There are just as many cruel masters and just as many abject slaves, even on our dear American soil, as there have ever been in the history of the world. Do you wonder what I mean? Are you inclined to question the truth of my statement? Not long ago I was made to realize more than ever before what it means to be a modern slave.

Once I had among my high-school pupils a boy of twenty. The first day of school I noticed that he had trouble with his mathematical problems. It seemed impossible for him to be accurate even when he seemed to understand perfectly how a problem should be solved. I thought there must be a cause for this, and I immediately began to watch him closely. I soon discovered the source of his trouble. Do you wonder what it was? I found that he was smoking a pipe, chewing tobacco, and *smoking cigarets*. At the end of a few days the boy seemed very much discouraged with his progress in school. As I had already won his confidence and made him feel that I was his friend, I thought it would be a good plan to have a talk with him and tell him frankly and kindly what was hindering his progress. One day I had him remain after I had dismissed the other pupils, and had a talk with him that I shall never forget.

He seemed very much surprized to learn that I had discovered a habit of which he was very much ashamed. I talked to him in a way that touched his heart, and with tears in his eyes he confessed that he *knew* he was injuring himself by using tobacco, but that he *could not* quit it. He had begun the habit when he was a small, motherless boy, and had continued it constantly since that time. Physicians had told him that the smoking of cigarets was very seriously injuring his heart, and would eventually kill him, and yet he sadly said, *"I can't quit."* Poor boy! I encouraged him all I could, and he made several desperate efforts to break the awful habit, but each time after a few days he would *have* to begin smoking again—so strong was the craving.

Not long after school began he was taken seriously ill and lay for weeks suffering from heart-trouble caused by the use of cigarets. He finally recovered, but I feel sure that unless the Lord saves him and breaks the chain of habit which binds him so tightly he will yet fill an early grave.

Do you not think that boy is as truly a slave as the poor slave chained to his oars? Is he not bound with chains which he can not break? Has he not a cruel, relentless master?

Dear boys and girls, I trust that none of you are bound by the chain of evil habits. Are you bound by even a tiny cord? You may think you can break the tiny cord, but listen: "Habit is a cable; every day we weave a thread, and soon we can not break it.'' We can not afford to weave the first thread. It is our sweet privilege to be free.

Are you already a slave? Have you a cruel master from whom you can not free yourself? Take heart; be encouraged. Jesus is waiting and longing ''to proclaim liberty to the captives, and the opening of the prison to them that are bound.''   —*Nellie Robinson Chute.*

A LESSON FROM THE GOAT

IF YOU will take a good look at the next goat you see you will discover that the corners of his mouth turn up, but never down, as if he were in a good humor all the time. This funny mouth with the turned-up corners, and the merry gray eyes, give him a most comical expression. He is apparently one of the most contented of all animals. If grass is plentiful he eats and is glad. If there is nothing to nibble he just climbs on the top of a rock or rail fence and looks pleasant. It is said that he can manage to pick up a meal where a mouse would starve, often helping himself to rubber shoes and titbits from an ashheap. Turn him into a lot that appears to be as bare as your hand, and in a few minutes he will be munching something, his eyes still twinkling and the corners of his mouth still pointing upward. If people who have formed a habit of giving way to a bad temper would smile more and look on the bright side of life they would be far happier and would shed sunshine wherever they go.

RULES FOR TALKING

CHOOSE to listen rather than to talk, for silence is preferable to speech.

It is wiser to talk too little than too much, and to speak well than to say many things.

Aim at speaking rather to the purpose than often.

Reflect before speaking.

Restrain the tongue when the heart is agitated.

Be silent when you feel too great a desire to talk.

Speak after others; never against others; always well of others.

Never seek information through curiosity.

Leave it to the world to talk of the world.

Complain of nothing, neither of persons or of things.

Say little of your works, less of your troubles; confide these but to few persons.

Utter no useless words. —*Selected.*

A GENTLEMAN

I knew him for a gentleman
By signs that never fail.
His coat was rough and rather worn,
His cheeks were thin and pale—
A lad who had his way to make,
With little time to play.
I knew him for a gentleman
By certain signs today.

He met his mother on the street;
Off came his little cap.
My door was shut; he waited there
Until I heard his rap.
He took the bundle from my hand,
And when I dropped my pen
He sprang to pick it up for me,
This gentleman of ten.

He does not push or crowd along;
His voice is gently pitched;
He does not fling his books about
As if he were bewitched.
He stands aside to let you pass;
He always shuts the door;
He runs on errands willingly,
To forge and mill and store.

He thinks of you before himself;
He serves you if he can,
For in whatever company,
The manners make the man.
At ten or forty 'tis the same—
The manner tells the tale;
And I discern the gentleman
By signs that never fail.

—*Selected.*

A BAD EFFECT

THERE is nothing in the world that will bring about your ruin any sooner than keeping bad company. Thousands of innocent boys and girls have been led away from the paths of right into a life of sin and sorrow because they associated with those whom they knew were not fit to be their companions. They were first influenced to do little things that were wrong, such as disobeying, telling lies, stealing some almost worthless articles, using bad language, smoking, fighting, playing cards, and many other things. As time went on they began to do worse things, and so the company they kept led them on deeper and deeper into sin, until their lives are wrecked and ruined.

Be very careful what kind of company you keep. . Shun evil companions, for they are sure to have a great influence over you, and though you escape the complete ruination of your life and character, you can not possibly escape injury. If you would be possessor of a noble and true character, seek the companionship of those whose lives are such as would influence you to always stand by the right and strive to put down everything of an evil nature. This class of companions will inspire you to a higher and nobler life, and thus you will prepare yourself for future usefulness.

There is a saying, "It is better to be alone than in bad company." You had better have no companions at all than to associate with those who would lead you away from God and right into a life of sin and despair, only to wreck your life and ruin your happiness. Be true to yourself and to your loved ones by shunning evil associates and bad company.   —*Nathan C. McNeill.*

WHY DOESN'T MOTHER SING?

"MAMA doesn't sing any more." These words were spoken by a sweet, blue-eyed girl, who, on account of her loving disposition and thoughtful ways, held, perhaps, a warmer place in her mother's heart than any of the other children.

Sister thought it over. It was true. Mother didn't sing as often as she did formerly. How they used to love to hear her singing in the kitchen, here and there, everywhere about the house! True, she did not know much about music and could not keep the tune very well, but there was something about her singing that made the children feel happy. The house was full of little ones, and there was work to be

done from early morning until late at night; but when Mother sang, the children knew that Jesus was blessing her soul.

But now Mother did not sing. The boys were about grown; the girls were one by one developing into young womanhood. Perhaps some of them were not as thoughtful of Mother as they should have been. Her cares and responsibilities were increasing. The toil of many years had left its stamp, and her body was becoming more and more feeble. Ah! little wonder that she did not feel so much like singing now.

Has your mother ceased to sing? If so, why has she? Perhaps by a little more thoughtfulness and kindness on your part you may again bring those songs to her lips.

Have you a singing mother in your home? Learn to appreciate her and be thoughtful of her, lest the cares and sorrows of life cause her voice to be hushed and her singing to cease. May you not have to say, "Mother doesn't sing any more." If you scatter sunshine and happiness along her pathway you may continue to hear her cheery voice praising God in song even though her body may be bent and her hair be silvery gray.   —*Contributed.*

WHAT A DAUGHTER CAN DO

THERE is so much a daughter can do for her mother that it is hard to know where to begin. Suppose we start with how she can help with the housework and care of the younger children.

For years the mother has had entire charge of both, and it is time she was relieved. Patiently and uncomplainingly she has drudged along with no thoughts except for her children's welfare and comfort. It should be the daughter's joy, as well as duty, to bring a little recreation and pleasure into her mother's life. Remember, girls, that all your lives your mothers have been sacrificing themselves for you. Now you have a chance to reverse things. Your shoulders are young and strong; help lift the burden a little from the tired shoulders that have borne it so long. Let mother see that you appreciate all that she has done for you. Take the heaviest part of the housework off her hands. Make her stay in bed in the morning while you get the breakfast. Send her out to enjoy herself while you look after the children. Of course, you can not do this every day, but you can do your share of it.

Confide in her and tell her your hopes and ambitions. She is better than all the girl friends in the world and will never tell your secrets.

The trouble about mothers is, that we get so used to them that we don't half appreciate them until we lose them. Then quickly enough we realize what all that divine care and tenderness meant. No matter how much you do, you can't begin to return all they have done for you, but do the best you can.

A little loving and petting are always appreciated by mothers; try it with yours and see if she does not thrive under it.

As for the girls who talk and act disrespectfully toward their mothers, for them no criticism is too harsh. If they only knew what outsiders think of it, I believe they would stop it. The prettiest girl in the world is absolutely devoid of charm if she is impertinent to her mother.

Begin today, girls, and save your mothers all the worries you can; show them all the consideration you can, and give them all the love you can. —*Selected.*

WISE SAYINGS OF LINCOLN

"IN REGARD to this handsome Bible presented to me, I have but to say it is the best gift God has given to man. But for it we could not know right from wrong. All things most desirable for man's welfare here and hereafter are to be found portrayed in it."

"Truth is your truest friend no matter what the circumstances are."

"The leading rule for the man in every calling is Diligence. Leave nothing for tomorrow which can be done today. Whatever piece of business you have in hand, before stopping do all the labor pertaining to it which can be done."

"I am not bound to win, but I am bound to be true. I am not bound to succeed, but I am bound to live up to what light I have."

"The way for a young man to rise is to improve himself every way he can, never suspecting that anybody wishes to hinder him. Suspicion and jealousy never did help any man in any situation. There may sometimes be ungenerous attempts to keep a young man down, and they will succeed, too, if he allows his mind to be diverted from the true channel to brood over the attempted injury. Cast about and see if this feeling has not injured every person you have ever known to fall into it."

LOLA BEEBE'S FAULT

"MRS. BEEBE, I have come to talk with you about Lola, for I am sure you always want to be a help to her," said Miss Barnes, Lola's teacher, one evening after she was comfortably settled in the easy chair that had been offered her in the cheerful little front room of the Beebe home.

"What is the matter? Has my little girl been naughty in school?" anxiously asked Mrs. Beebe, for she much desired that her children do right.

"Lola is a good child and a good pupil; she studies hard and advances well; but she has been overtaken in a fault lately that I am not able to help her see. It is something which, I fear, will affect her whole life if it is neglected; so I have come to you, believing you will help me to get the child to understand the seriousness of her fault.

"The other day we were having a test in arithmetic, and I happened to notice Lola's paper after she had handed it to a classmate for correction, and one of the answers was wrong. Later when it was handed to me it was right, the figures having been altered so that the problem had the right answer. In itself it amounts to little, but the principle is wrong. If she is made to see it now, it will help her to be honest all her life.

"I have talked with Lola several times about it, and each time she stoutly denies that she changed the figures. I am sure I am not mistaken, so I have come to you. You understand me, Mrs. Beebe—the incident in itself has no weight except the influence on the character of your child."

While Miss Barnes explained the trouble, Mrs. Beebe sat listening closely, glad indeed in her heart that she had her child entrusted to the care of one so careful and conscientious. She was sorry that Lola had been overcome with such a fault; for, above all other things, she had tried to impress upon her children the beauty of honesty and truthfulness. She felt no resentment towards the teacher who had come to her with this complaint, but counseled with her as to the best way to help Lola.

That night when Lola was safe in her little bed and all the other children were asleep, Mrs. Beebe slipped in to her bed and began talking to her about her trouble at school, but Lola again denied as firmly as before that she had altered the figures. She maintained that she was wrongly accused and that Miss Barnes was doing her an injustice to insist that she had changed the answer. Mrs. Beebe was much disappointed, for she had expected Lola to confess at once what she had done. She left her alone for that night, but in the morning she had another quiet talk with her about it. When Lola arrived at school Miss Barnes expected to hear her confess her dishonesty, and had another talk with her, but still the girl firmly denied, as at first.

It would have been easy to let the matter drop then, but the teacher was so sure she was not mistaken that the more Lola denied it, the worse the fault became. Not a day passed that she did not seek opportunity to speak to Lola about the altered figures and ask her if she had not changed the answer.

Mrs. Beebe was of the same mind, and morning and night she talked with Lola about it. The matter was kept before the child for one week, yet without any sign of surrender on Lola's part.

"Lola, did you have a talk with Miss Barnes today about that answer, and did you tell her just how it was?" Mrs. Beebe would ask gently.

"Mama, I did not alter those figures, and I can not say that I did. Miss Barnes thinks I did, but she is mistaken," Lola would answer.

"Lola, are you sure you did not? Remember God hears you, and he knows if you are not telling the truth. It was wrong for you to change the figures, but it was worse for you to deny it."

"I did not change that answer; I never changed a single figure," the little girl would say stoutly.

But things were getting desperate for the little girl. She had observed other children do just what she had done, and she had not known of their being spoken to about it; then, why should the teacher and her mother make such a fuss because she had changed a few figures? She had known how to work the problem, and had only made a mistake that she could alter very easily. What difference did it make, any way? She had done nothing more than every one else did, she thought; then, why should she be so singled out?

But the better part of Lola's nature rebelled against her deception, and reasoned thus: "Maybe it was wrong for me to do that. Perhaps Mama and Teacher are right. It is terribly wicked for me to say I did not when I did."

Finally the good prevailed, and she wept out her confession on

Mama's breast. They both felt better after it was all confessed. How different she felt with that load of guilt off her little heart!

The next day she confessed to Miss Barnes also that she had been telling an untruth about it, and then the trouble was ended.

Lola was then in the third grade, but in after-years when she was in a much higher grade and when she was nearly grown, she confided to her mother that that experience had helped her to do honest work through all her school-life.   —*Mabel Hale.*

A BIT OF GOOD ADVICE

HERE are a few words of advice spoken by a father to his son on the evening of the son's graduation from Yale University: "My boy, your life is before you. All the years of accomplishment are not behind you—they are before you. Whatever you do, stick to your ideals. Never do a thing you refuse to look a man in the face for. Stand firm. Make every sacrifice you desire, but do not sell yourself."

"The boy or girl who can face ridicule, and stand by what he or she knows to be right, and who is not to be morally stampeded by any one's laugh, scoff, or sneer, is a person of whom splendid things may be expected."

"True greatness, if it be anywhere on earth, is in a private virtue, removed from the notion of pomp and vanity."

POISON IN BOOKS

ONE DAY a gentleman in India took from his library shelf a book. As he did so he felt at the end of one finger a little pain like that caused by the prick of a pin. He thought that a pin had been left in the book as a bookmark and began reading. Soon his finger began to swell, then his arm, then his whole body, and in a few days he died. The pain in his finger was not from a pin but from a small deadly serpent which had housed itself in the leaves of the book.

If the tiny green deadly snakes of India were the only serpents that nestled among the books, we could guard against them, but they are not. There are thousands of poisonous snake-thoughts in books of the present time. They are so artfully coiled and so snugly concealed that often their presence is unknown, their sting unfelt, until the "book is finished" and laid down. Multitudes have exclaimed after the poison had begun to work, "Oh, if I had never read that book!"

—Selected.

SOME THINGS A SCHOOLBOY SHOULD KNOW

MY SUBJECT no doubt has brought to your minds arithmetic, geography, history, and other studies which a boy is expected to learn at school. To be sure, you should learn how to apply the principles of arithmetic, so that you may deal with figures cleverly; you should learn of the size and motions of the earth, its natural divisions, its climate, and the distribution of plants and animals, and of men, their customs, industrial pursuits, and forms of governments; you should learn of voyage and discovery, of colonial life, of wars and great generals—you should learn of all these things and many others; but these are not the things I wish to speak of in particular.

I wish to notice some of the qualities that a boy must possess in order to make the best of his opportunities.

First, he must be regular and prompt in attendance. The boy who comes to school five days in the week and is found in his place each morning ready for opening exercises has more than double the chance for an education that a boy has who is present three days in a week and is ten or fifteen minutes late when he does come. It is said that the early bird catches the worm. Much is gained by regular and prompt attendance.

Then, second, he must be attentive. The chief reason why pupils do not remember better is that they do not give fixed attention to what they hear or read. Some time ago a certain teacher read to her class an experience of Benjamin Franklin with electricity and asked them to reproduce the account as an exercise in composition. This is what she read:

"Every one has noticed that the fur on a cat's back, when stroked vigorously the wrong way, will send out electric sparks. Franklin asked himself, Are these sparks the same as the flashes of lightning seen in a thunder-storm? He resolved to find out. To do this he sent up a kite during a shower and fastened a door-key near the end of the string. Touching his knuckle to the key, he got an electric spark from it. This

and other experiences convinced him that his conjecture was right; electricity and lightning, he said, are one and the same thing."

Now I will give a copy of a composition written as a reproduction of what was read:

"Benjamin Franklin best known things was electricity. So one day when it came up a storm he flew up a kite with a key fastened on the end of the string, and then he touched his knuckles on the key. But he didn't find any different in it and the cat. He taken a cat when it was cold weather and taken it into a dark room and rubbed it and the electricity would just fly."

Do you not think that a lack of attention to what was read was the cause of this pupil's poor composition?

Third, to be successful, a boy must apply himself diligently to his studies. The one who thinks more of baseball and other sports and makes them the principal object of school, or likes to sit around the fireside and listen to stories rather than study the lessons assigned for the next day, will not make a success of his school-work.

Remember the race of the tortoise and the hare. The tortoise kept on plodding, but the hare lay down by the roadside and slept. While the hare was sleeping the tortoise reached the goal.

There are other qualities I might mention, such as neatness, accuracy, etc., which go toward making a boy successful in his work at school.

And these very qualities that tend to make a boy a success as a student, will bring success to him in mature years. He will be a better business man, a better citizen, and a better Christian because of the punctuality, diligence, attentiveness, neatness, accuracy, etc., he cultivates when a boy.   —*Leonora Insley Pendleton.*

SOME WISE SAYINGS

THE SECRET of success is constancy to purpose.—*Disraeli.*

There is no excellence without great labor.—*Wm. Wirt.*

There is no time in life when books do not influence a man.—*Besant.*

It matters not how a man dies, but how he lives.—*Samuel Johnson.*

An investment in knowledge always pays the best interest.—*Franklin.*

The measure of a man's life is the well spending of it, and not the length.—*Plutarch*.

How poor are they that have not patience.—*Shakespeare*.

Never promise more than you can perform.—*Publius Syrus*.

Dost thou love life? Then do not squander time, for that is the stuff life is made of.—*Franklin*.

Whatever is worth doing at all, is worth doing well.—*Chesterfield*.

Few things are impossible to diligence and skill.—*Samuel Johnson*.

COULDN'T AND COULD

Couldn't and Could were two promising boys
  Who lived not a great while ago.
They had just the same playmates and just the same toys,
And just the same chances for winning life's joys
  And all that the years may bestow.

And Could soon found out he could fashion his life
  On lines very much as he planned;
He could cultivate goodness and guard against strife,
  And win with the watchword, "I can!"
He could have all his deeds with good cheer to be rife,
  And build him a name that would stand.

But poor little Couldn't just couldn't pull through;
  All the trials he met with a sigh;
When a task needed doing, he couldn't, he knew;
And hence, when he couldn't, how could he? Could you
  If you couldn't determine you'd try?

So Could just kept building his way to success,
  Nor clouding his sky with a doubt;
But Couldn't strayed into the Slough of Distress.
Alas! and his end is easy to guess—
  Strayed in, but he couldn't get out.

And that was the difference 'twixt Couldn't and Could:
  Each followed his own chosen plan;
And when Couldn't just wouldn't, Could earnestly would,
And where one of them weakened the other "made good,"
  And won with his watchword, "I can!"

—*Selected*.

WHAT HE COULD DO

A LITTLE boy in Boston, rather small for his years, worked in an office as an errand boy for four gentlemen, who occupied desks there. One day the men were chaffing him a little about being so small and said to him, "You will never amount to much; you can never do much business, you are too small."

The little fellow looked at them. "Well," said he, "small as I am, I can do something which none of you four men can do."

"Ah! what is it?" they asked.

"I don't know that I ought to tell you," he replied.

But they were anxious to know and urged him to tell what he could do that none of them were able to do.

At last the little fellow solemnly answered, "I can keep from swearing!"

UP, NOT DOWN

Nay! Manhood Street winds up, not down.
  Eyes to the front, my lad;
Shoulders square and heart brave and true,
Facing whatever may come to you
  Or whatever the road, my lad.

Whether it's cloudy or whether bright,
  Whistle a bit the day;
Whether it's morning or whether night,
  Marching along the way,
Throw up your head, throw wide your heart,
  Hold out a hand on the road;
The minute you've helped a traveler,
  You have gained a hundredfold.

There are men and then men, my laddie;
  And some of them, I ween,
Are after the heart of their Maker,
  And others I have seen
Are not quite up to the standard
  It takes to fashion a man.
So, my lad, as you're toiling upward,
  Reach a goal that gleams high, if you can!
                              —*Beacon.*

A WESTERN PRODIGAL

Chapter I

"I'LL leave home, then, sir. I won't be held down by such iron-clad rules," muttered a young man, whom we shall call Clifton Craig, to his father as they stood in the back yard of their home, where for some time they had been engaged in earnest conversation.

"I am very sorry, my son, that you are deciding as you are," replied the father; "but your mother and I have thoroughly considered this matter, and we can not change. If you were the only child in our home, Clifton, it might make some difference in regard to this last consideration; but you can understand, I believe, that we are forced to be very scrupulous in the matter of home-principle for the sake of the younger children."

"It's settled, then," and Clifton Craig turned from his father and entered the house.

Just the day before, Mrs. Craig was informed that Clifton had attended a dance, and in the evening she and her husband had a serious consultation and decided that Mr. Craig should speak to the son.

On leaving his father, Clifton first went to his mother with a faint hope of gaining some advantage there.

"I have promised to go to a dance tomorrow night, Mother, and told Father I would not go to another if he would consent to my going this time. He will not permit even that; so I intend to leave home."

This was a hard test for mother sympathy. Many thoughts flashed through Mrs. Craig's mind in the few minutes that her son stood waiting for a reply. "If we let him go to only this one he will not leave home," she mused while her heart yearned for her son. "If I speak to my husband he may change his mind." "What would you do if the boy should happen to his death at such a place, which has been the fate of some young men?" interrupted a warning voice. "Can you consent to your son's committing a sin, and remain irresponsible yourself?" No, no! she could not bear the thought of the guilt before her God. Promptly she answered aloud, while tears filled her tender, loving eyes:

"My dear son, my heart is filled with sorrow; but I feel that your father is in the right, and I shall stand by what he has said. Reconsider your decision and heed his instructions."

Clifton was much affected; but, without saying another word, he turned away and immediately left the room. His own eyes were filled and his voice choked beyond utterance.

In many ways Clifton was a good boy, and he had a fondness for home; so it was a pity that he was taking this fatal step. Like many others of his age, he was resenting home rule, not realizing that his future as well as his present happiness and success depended on a proper submission rather than on haughty independence. And like others, he did not realize that reverence for parents and their instruction is a wise and noble quality in a young man or woman.

Clifton went up to his room and began looking over his wardrobe and other possessions. "I can't change now," he said to himself. "Since I've said it, I'll be a man and stick to it." He braced himself and began vigorously brushing and packing his clothing.

When the children heard of their brother's intention their grief was pitiful. The little ones were crying and clinging to their mother, who also was weeping silently. Ida, the oldest, was scolding and crying, hardly knowing whom to blame, her father and mother, or her brother.

"Mama, Mama, will Clifton ever come back?" pleaded little Gladys.

"No; he won't, and he'll get bad and gamble and drink," spoke up Ida indignantly. "You'll never see Brother again if he leaves home now," she added, growing more and more excited.

"O-o-h!" wailed the heart-broken little sister, burying her face in her mother's lap, while baby Mabel cried louder through sympathy, although she was not old enough yet to understand it all.

"Be more composed, children. God is a help in every trouble. Let us trust him to bring Brother back to us by and by," spoke the tender mother soothingly.

When Clifton came down-stairs, there was still a suggestion of moisture and redness about his eyes, but he spoke with a forced cheerfulness.

"I'll not take my guitar, Mother. And you girls may have these trinkets," he said, tossing them on the center-table. "I think I shall leave the trunk, too, if you have no objections. I can send for it later if I want it—or I might come back some day," he added, dropping his voice a little.

"All right, son. Leave anything you like."

"Ida, you may take lessons on the guitar, if you will be very careful with it," he said comfortingly as he saw his dear sister standing by the window sobbing.

He wanted to say more; but, not knowing just what would be appropriate, he slipped back up-stairs, for Ida was too much broken up to make any reply or even to thank him for the offer, which she would have greatly appreciated under any other circumstances. He was soon dressed in his best suit—a dark-blue serge, a light silk necktie, patent oxfords, a broadcloth overcoat, and a beaver hat.

Clifton was an industrious young man, and he had been saving with his money, seldom using more than was needed for clothes, though occasionally making a rather generous gift to parents or sisters. Now, as he viewed himself in the mirror, then thought of the coin in his pocket, he felt a swelling of boyish pride and of satisfaction with himself. He possessed full confidence in his ability to "make it easy in the world." But he had never been far from home, and, being well acquainted in his home community, he had not found any difficulty in obtaining work. The broad world is not to be judged by our little home village with its few hundred friendly, open-hearted inhabitants.

No cloud of stern reality flitted across the clear blue sky of imagination for our young prodigal, and every warning voice was instantly hushed as he stepped forth on this bright December morning full of strength, hope, and courage. Even the farewell to the old home, parents, and sisters amid cries and sobs was not enough to move him from his resolution, so confident was he of future success and happiness. But his mother's parting words smote him. At first they were a goad that urged him forward; then, as he became convinced that the providence of God was against him, they became a soothing, beseeching voice calling him to return to home and rest.

"Remember, Son, that wherever you go, Father's and Mother's prayers will follow you. God will not forget you, although it may sometimes not be in a way you might wish. You will be welcomed at any time you may decide to return, only you know on what conditions."

"Yes, so we both say. Good-by," added the father, and he affectionately clasped his son in his arms just as he used to do when Clifton was a little lad.

It was almost too much for the boy, but he shook off that which he called "babyishness" and boldly stepped forth.

"I'll write, Mother," he called back at a slight turn in the road as he saw her still standing in the doorway wiping her tearful eyes.

When he had gone far enough that he thought he was out of sight he set his valise down on the ground and took a long parting look at the old home. As he looked, he almost wavered. Never had the house and grounds seemed so homelike, the hills so green and beautiful, the little town just beyond so quiet and peaceful. All seemed to be inviting him to stay. Memory took him flying backward to his boyhood days—days of joyous innocence at home and school.

As he stood lost in retrospection, he was suddenly awakened to his surroundings by Rover, his dog, who came bounding down the road toward him.

"Rover, old boy, you must go back. I can't take you on this trip," he said, as he stooped down and affectionately patted the head of his comrade and play-fellow of boyhood days. "Go back now, Rover, and take good care of Mother and baby Mabel."

Poor Rover was disappointed. Dropping his ears and tail, he walked slowly toward the house, occasionally looking back to be sure his master intended he should go on. Clifton watched the dog, urging him on whenever he looked backward, until he reached a turn in the road and was hidden from view by the fencecorner. Then slowly taking up his valise, Clifton went on to the station.

For a long time the young man had greatly desired to see the coast. Portland, specially, had figured largely in his youthful fancies. Now was his opportunity to realize his dreams. Accordingly, he purchased a ticket and took the first train for Portland, Ore.

Chapter II

CLIFTON arrived in Portland early in the morning. The wind was blowing and the rain coming down in torrents.

"Not a very pleasant day for sightseeing," he said to his companion in the seat opposite, with whom he had formed a hasty friendship.

"Plenty of 'sights' indoors until the rain is over," his companion replied. "Here we are," he added as the train slowed down. "Come on. I'll show you our great city."

A wiser young man would have shunned a chance acquaintance that made himself so familiar; but this village lad was charmed with this same friendliness and thought himself very fortunate in having made the acquaintance of one so advanced, as compared with himself, in knowledge, especially knowledge of the city he had long wished to visit and had now entered. This new friend was a few years Clifton's senior, jovial, talkative, obliging, and very entertaining.

Of course, the first place to be visited was a lunch-room. The young men were hungry. They ate heartily and conversed freely. They talked mostly about amusements and sports. Wilford Jones, Clifton's companion, knew all the game-houses, the play-houses, and the ale-houses.

"Let's go across the street and get a little to drink, and have a game of cards," he suggested.

"I never drink," said Clifton, wishing to add, "and would rather not play cards," but courage failed there.

Clifton followed this leader, whose steps led downward, yet all the time his conscience drew hard on its tender strings. This was not the side of Portland he had intended to see; but what could he do? He dared not separate himself entirely from this man yet; for loneliness forbade his parting from the only one in this large city whom he knew. He dared not tell this jolly, care-free fellow that he had decided not to play another game of cards, that he had been reared by Christian parents, that he was the son of a minister. No, the same old question, "What would he think?" prevented this. And so Clifton followed on.

"What do you play?" asked Wilford, as they took seats at a table.

"I'm not a very good player. You'd better get some one else to play with you," ventured Clifton.

"No; come on, you'll soon learn if you play with me. You'll make an expert, Craig."

After several weeks of this following the butterfly, conscience ceased to talk so loudly as at first, and our Clifton seemed to be having a very enjoyable time. Portland was a charming city of pleasure. Every one was so friendly. He was flattered into thinking he was one of the most popular in the set of which he had now become a member. Every fellow seemed to vie in doing him honor for a season; but later he found that these were mostly designing men and that when his money was gone their friendship also had flown. The little pile of savings that his youthful fancy had imagined as almost inexhaustible, he suddenly awoke to realize was nearly gone. Nights and days of pleasureseeking and gaming rob one of health, wealth, and moral life. As he began to realize these conditions, memory and conscience awoke.

When he went to his room for rest and sleep after such revelry, sleep did not come at once. Shame and remorse lashed him in their turn. Memory brought visions of home, and imagination pictured the old familiar scene of the family around the home circle. There was Father reading from that Book which Clifton had learned to reverence from babyhood; there was Mother—was ever another mother like her, so good and kind?—and baby Mabel on Mother's knee; Ida and Gladys erect and attentive to the Bible story. The story that night, he fancied, was of the prodigal, and every one was sad; for the story had a living significance. Now they bowed to pray. He could almost, it seemed, hear their voices; for he was sure of what and for whom they were all praying. Even little Mabel, who could not yet speak plainly, lisped a prayer. "Dod, bess Bover. Bring 'im home soon." So they all prayed—"God bless our wandering son and brother"—and God heard their prayers. During those still hours of the night, in that lonely room, He visited that wayward heart.

"You are not satisfied, son," the Spirit whispered. "You do not enjoy this life, for there is no true pleasure in it. Return to your home and loved ones. Return to your God, who will wash away all these spots and give you perfect rest and true pleasure. Why will you any longer grieve the heart of your loving parents for folly? See, your character is gone, your money is nearly gone, and your health is in great danger. You are gaining nothing, but losing so much. Besides all this, you are forming habits that will, unless broken soon, bind you as fast as a captive's chains. Arise, my son, arise! Free yourself from this life and these evil associates. Hesitate no longer!"

"Yes; it is true I am not happy at all. I am losing everything. And I see that those fellows are not so attentive and friendly since my money does not come so freely. Besides that, they are low, and, what is worse, I am becoming like them. I will leave them at once; but I can not go home yet. I must make some money and straighten my life first."

Before he fell asleep that night, he planned to take an early train the next morning for the Gray's Harbor country.

When Clifton arrived in the town of Hoquiam and sought employ-ment, nothing was available but work in the woods. Even there luck was still against him. Only two men were desired for a certain job, and, singular as it may seem, two others had already been hired. The three young men got together and agreed to work by turns.

Everything went well for a time. Wages and weather were fine; the boys were good-natured, obliging fellows; and Clifton congratulated himself on his good luck.

But one morning the two boys complained of feeling "bum" and did not want to go to work with the rest.

"You may have the job today, Craig," said the eldest. "We're going to town."

"Be back at noon?" he asked.

"Not likely. It's easier lying around town than around this old shack."

Clifton went off with the rest of the crew to work without a foreboding of evil. At noon nobody thought it strange that the boys had not returned; but when supper was past and bedtime had come and still they had not been seen nor heard from, some expressed themselves as fearing that the boys had really become sick. While the men in the bunk-house were discussing the advisability of sending a man to town the next day if the boys had not arrived by noon, Clifton suddenly exclaimed:

"A thief's been here! My things are all gone. Just look at this, boys!"

Exclamations of surprize and disgust burst from many lips as the men beheld the scattered letters and pictures, and perceived that the boy's fine leather suit-case, of which he had been so particular, and all it held of any intrinsic value, including that blue serge suit, shoes, and hat, and also the broadcloth overcoat that had been hanging above, had disappeared. Truly this was a great disappointment.

No one wanted to accuse the boys. They had seemed to be such good, quiet fellows. But the cook must be questioned, for he would likely know if any stranger had been around during work-hours. No; he had seen no one around during the day. He saw the boys go away in the morning about nine o'clock. Yes, one of them had a suit-case, and he was quite sure that the other had an overcoat thrown across his arm; but that was nothing peculiar or strange, for men are always coming and going at a lumber-camp, although few of them, it is true, bring valuables or fine clothes to a camp.

There was little room for further doubt as to where the guilt lay, but as to the remedy for the disappointment, there seemed none. The culprits had doubtless been out of the country many hours.

Poor Clifton! For a long time he lay in deep thought. He was not prospering; that surely was true. He would like to go home at once; but how could he go like this! He counted his wages. Tomorrow was pay-day. By careful calculations, he decided there would be enough to fit himself with a cheap outfit and to buy his ticket for home. But the shame at the thought of the change since he left a few months before caused him to decide to work yet another month.

The following day was Saturday. The men were paid in the evening after work. As they filed into the little office one by one and out again, each face wore an expression of satisfaction. Clifton was the last one in the line. His feet lagged. They had lagged all day. Besides his recent disappointment, he had not the encouraging anticipation of a large check, as the others had. He had been hired late in the month and had been able to work only part of the time since that. He did not step forward with the hope and the eagerness that characterized the others. The paymaster seemed not to notice Clifton; for his eyes were down. He closed the books and looked up.

"You haven't written my check, Green," Clifton said.

"Your check! I wrote it yesterday. Didn't the boys divide that with you? You know the way you fellows hired out; I couldn't write but two checks for the two jobs. But you three agreed to divide the time and the money between yourselves, and so they said yesterday that you sent them in to the town-office while you held down the job, and that they would divide with you. I'm truly sorry for you, Craig," he added as the poor boy walked slowly away without answering a word.

Disappointment would not express Clifton Craig's bitterness of soul. At first he felt resentful towards the boys; then he saw it was his own fault.

"I'm a fool for leaving a good home and a good position to drag out my life like this. When I left home four months ago, I had good clothes and plenty of money. Today I haven't a decent garment, own nothing in the world but my watch, haven't even money enough to take me home. But I'm going, anyway; enough of this!" he said emphatically as he straightened up and perceived that his feet had involuntarily followed the road and that he was moving in the direction of the town and railroad station. He quickened his pace while his mind became alert and encouraged at the thought of home.

Chapter III

ON REACHING the station, Clifton found his train, a freight, would be due in about an hour. Hurriedly getting himself some supper, he went back to the ticket-office to purchase a ticket. But since he must have something to eat on the way, he dared not spend all his money for a ticket. He bought as far as he thought he dared, however, and boarded the freight-train at 7:45.

His destination, according to his ticket, was a little town in the mountains. The snow there was yet several inches deep, and a mixture of rain and snow was falling. So walking was very difficult and disagreeable. Having noticed how some others beat their way on the train, Clifton decided to make a venture. He had ridden almost to the foot of the mountains on the homeward side when the brakeman discovered him and ordered him off the train. Cold and shivering, hungry and discouraged, he set out on foot for the next village.

There was nothing whatever to give him an idea of the distance. After walking about two miles and just before nightfall, he came in view of that welcome sight—a town. On making inquiries as to the remaining distance home, he calculated that there was enough in his scanty purse to warrant his risking the price of a good meal and a bed for the night. "If I must beg, it will be when I have no money," he said to himself.

He continued walking for three days. By this time his money had dwindled to a few cents, and he had even begged for two meals—a humiliating experience, although he had been treated with due kindness.

Late in the afternoon he saw on his way a fine-looking farmhouse. "I'll ask to chop wood there for a supper, and perhaps I may help with the chores and get a bed." As Clifton opened the garden-gate a savage-looking dog came bounding out to meet him. A woman stuck her head through the kitchen-door to call back the dog, but on seeing Clifton demanded roughly:

"What do you want here?"

"Have you any work that I could do to earn a little to eat?"

" 'To eat!' I should say not! We have nothing to throw away on tramps."

Clifton began to explain, but was rudely interrupted.

"Leave here at once, or I'll set that dog on you!"

The prospects of spending a night by himself and on the ground were not at all pleasing; but as he walked on several miles farther without seeing another farmhouse and as night was falling, this seemed to be the only thing left to do. Finding a somewhat sheltered nook on the protected side of the grade, he made a little fire with a few sticks and lumps of coal he had gathered along the railroad after leaving the farm-house, and then, supperless, he sat down to wait for morning light.

Home was not far away now, but, agreeably with the proverb, "The darkest hour is just before dawn," our weary, lonely prodigal felt this night was the darkest. His own miserable, unworthy, sinful condition was an awful contrast to the picture that played constantly before his mind. The sweet comforts of home and of loving hearts, purity, righteousness, and peace shone luminous in this darkness.

He soon fell into an uneasy sleep. When he awoke, he was chilly and stiff. His fire was all burned out. He must arise and walk on. Possibly he should reach a farmhouse or a village before long, where he might find some friendly shelter.

He had not gone far when, on turning a curve in the track, he saw the lights of a town. Quickening his pace as best he could in the darkness, he pressed on more hopefully and reached the town just before a freight-train pulled in from the direction in which Clifton had just come. That meant a lift toward home.

On making inquiries as to the route of this train, Clifton learned it would pass through his town some time during the coming day, but would not stop, although it was expected to stop at the station just before. The brakeman, who was a kindly man, seeing the wistful expression of the boy's face asked as Clifton turned to leave him, "Want to ride?" and without waiting for an answer said, "Get aboard." The freight was soon pulling out.

.   .   .   .

At twilight, just as a little group were sitting down to their evening meal in an eastern Washington home, a young man in shabby and soiled woodsman's attire passed through the gate and came up the gravel walk to the kitchen-door. When he knocked, the door was timidly opened by a delicate little woman, who stepped slightly backward when she saw the stranger and noted his appearance.

"Are Mr. and Mrs. Craig at home?" he asked, courteously lifting his hat.

At this Ida Craig, who was not far behind the woman and eyeing the stranger critically, screamed "Clifton!" and ran toward her brother with outstretched arms. Gladys too, recognizing him now, jumped from her chair at the table, crying, "Brother! Brother!" and ran into his open arms as he stooped to receive her.

When the excitement had somewhat subsided it was explained that Mr. and Mrs. Craig had been called away for a short time to assist in a series of revival meetings and had left the two girls and the house in charge of an acquaintance. Clifton could not be contented long at home without seeing his father and mother. Having found in his room a suit that he had considered not worth taking on the previous journey, he now thankfully donned it and went to see his parents.

His coming was a grateful surprize. When he had privately and humbly rehearsed to them a detailed account of his wanderings and troubles, and had made a manly acknowledgement of his wrongs, his mother said: "Son, God is good to us! He it is who has brought you safely to us again. We could not pray that he would make your path smooth or easy, but that he should choose for you that which would cause you to return and repent. All he doeth is in love. We trust the lesson, though severe, is well learned."

"Do not fear, Mother. I shall never leave home in that way again. I have found that the world cares nothing for a fellow, but much for his money. Henceforth my parents' God shall be my God, and their people shall be my people." —*Anna M. Greeley.*